Trouble Isla

By

Lynda L. Lock

&

Dedication – Paradise Lost

Lawrie Lock: March 3rd 1942 – September 3rd 2018

Paradise is normally considered to be a place, but for me paradise is a person; my husband, adventure partner, world-traveler, lover and best friend - Lawrie Lock.

He was always my rock, my inspiration, my sounding board. We've traveled the world together getting into mischief, sticky situations and occasionally heated arguments that revolved around a finicky classic car doing something weird.

His recent diagnosis of Rapid Onset ALS caught us by surprise, and the speed with which Lawrie declined into complete paralysis took our breath away. But through it all he smiled that killer-gorgeous smile, and tried to make the best of a horrific situation. He slipped away on September 3rd 2018, at home, looking at the beautiful Caribbean Sea.

If the rain is liquid sunshine, then my tears are liquid love. I will love you to my last breath.

Chapter 1

December 31st 4:00 a.m.

The long sleek sport-fishing boat powered slowly backwards into a berth at the Bally Hoo wharf on Isla Mujeres. Her white hull and varnished decks glistened in the bright overhead security lights. A lean figure—dressed in khaki shorts, short-sleeved white shirt, and deck shoes—stepped onto the dock, wrapping the stern line around a bollard as the captain expertly settled the craft. The skipper cut the engines, removed the ignition key, and stepped away from the controls.

The deckhand's shaved pale head gleamed under the overhead lights, and his short beard looked recent, as if he hadn't shaved for a few days. Moving along the length of the boat, securing lines and placing heavy foam bumpers between the dock and the hull of the pricey yacht, the man looked competent and comfortable around the water. It was a ruse; he didn't know much at all about big yachts like this one, but he was a quick study.

According to the first mate, this baby was a classic; a beautifully maintained wooden yacht, custom-built on Harkers Island in North Carolina. Even a tiny scratch in the glossy finish would earn them an ear chewing from the boss.

The owners were due to fly in from Houston in time to celebrate New Year's Eve on the island. Then they were scheduled for a few weeks of deep-sea fishing, eating, and drinking before they returned to their home in Texas, leaving the captain and the two deckhands to bring their yacht back to its home berth at Seabrook Marina.

"It's still damn early, but I'll go ashore to see if anyone is available to process us through customs," the captain said, gathering up his waterproof document folder and stepping over the transom. "If not, I'll radio Cancun to tell them we're here and will check in later in the morning."

"Aye, aye Skipper," the man said, offering a two-fingered sardonic salute to the back of the departing captain.

"Jeff, wait up. I'll go with you and stretch my legs," the short red-haired man said as he nimbly hopped onto the docks. He turned to the man, "Frank, you okay to stay with her until we get back?"

The man, the one they knew as Frank, waved, "Sure Andy, take your time," he said. Remembering a humorous sign that he had seen in a bar on his previous visit to Isla Mujeres, he mumbled, "And thank you very *mucking futch* for the ride." It had been free transportation back to his hunting grounds.

It had been a busy three days for the man known as Frank. First, he had hitched a ride from Tampa to Houston with an accommodating long-haul truck driver. Behind a truckers' gas station, well away from the security cameras that were aimed at the fuel pumps, the body of the driver was now stinking up the cab of his rig. The driver's death had been unavoidable as soon as he had agreed to give the hitchhiker a lift to Texas. The passenger's clean-shaven image had been splashed across television news channels as one of the suspected fatalities in a fiery vehicle smash-up. Even though his appearance had changed with the beginning of a new beard and shaving off his dark hair, he couldn't risk leaving the driver alive. Most truckers were lonely gossips, and this one had been very talkative. In no time at all, he would be telling his buddies he had dropped off that same man in Houston.

It had then taken him another full day to scour the numerous marinas for a captain who was leaving shortly, heading to Isla Mujeres for the sport fishing season. The third day was eaten up with the voyage to the island.

Inside the main salon, Frank checked the time. If he remembered correctly from his previous visit to the island, he had seen the harbor master's office located a short walk south, close to the passenger ferry terminal. He probably had thirty to forty minutes tops, but at this hour of the morning it wasn't likely anyone would be available to do the paperwork, so the two men would probably be back in twenty minutes. Time to move.

He quickly walked to his berth and slipped on a dark nylon windbreaker, pulling a peaked cap down over his skull. Once the sun was up, he planned to wear a pair of dark sunglasses to hide his bright blue eyes.

A few minutes spent searching the other sleeping areas netted him about two hundred and fifty dollars in cash and a small Nikon camera that he might be able to pawn for a few bucks. He was owed a portion of that for the sixteen hours he had already worked, so he felt confident the men wouldn't try to find him for such a small amount.

The captain, Jeff Crompton, had hired him on for cash wages to be paid at the end of the two weeks, but he had never asked for identification or a passport. He supposed Crompton didn't really care if a deckhand was thrown in a Mexican jail for not having the proper paperwork. He could likely check around the gringo bars and hire another American, someone who wanted to work for a few weeks and have free transportation back to the States.

The blue-eyed man checked the time. *Gotta go. Things to do, scores to settle, and people to kill.*

Chapter 2

New Year's Eve 00:01 a.m.

Midnight. The fireworks exploded overhead, spraying the revelers with bits of flaming paper and hot shards from the shattered rocket casings. At five feet seven inches tall and wearing her favorite red stiletto heels, Yasmin Medina stood eye to eye with her new love, Carlos Mendoza. Just yesterday at the *Loco Lobo* Restaurant, she had discovered that Carlos, her good friend and boss, hungered for her. He had gently squeezed her hand and smiled as he gazed deeply into her green eyes. She had secretly lusted after this sexy man for over two years.

Carlos wrapped his arm around her slim waist, pulling Yasmin close. A faint scar running from his left eyebrow to the corner of his mouth was only noticeable because she knew it was there. A souvenir of his younger, reckless years.

"I'm going home now," he said. "Tomorrow will be a busy day feeding the hungry drunks at the restaurant." His eyes shining, he asked, "Come home with me?"

His sensual smile made her tremble, her insides turning to liquid fire. "*Mi amor*, I promised Jessica months ago that we would celebrate all night and then do the traditional greeting of the sunrise at Punta Sur." It was a long-standing island custom, one that her friend and co-worker, Jessica Sanderson, had yet to experience.

Carlos turned to look over at their lively group of friends. Jessica's cascade of long blonde curls was easy to pick out amongst the dark-haired locals. "Can't she find someone else to go with her? Why not Luis? He obviously has the hots for her."

"I promised," Yasmin said. The thumping beats from the eleven-person salsa band pounded in her eardrums and reverberated in her chest, making intimate conversations difficult.

"Okay," he nodded unhappily, accepting her decision. Then he crushed his lips to hers, kissing her long and deep, running his hands down the length of her back before he released her. "A little something to think about, *mi amor*, while you are dancing with the young boys." His voice held a hint of laughter, and his eyes were full of mischief.

"You are a devil, Carlos Mendoza." Yasmin said, as she slipped away from his arms. "I'll see you tomorrow at work."

Yasmin enjoyed the rear view as Carlos headed towards his car. He was whistling and twirling his keys around on a finger like an old-time gunfighter might spin his six-shooter before killing the bad guys. At thirty-nine years old, he had a trim, muscular build—and a great ass.

The tall man watched from a distance, twisting his head to track Carlos, then refocussing on the two women as they danced in a crush of whirling bodies. *Too many people, too many witnesses around the women*, he thought, and turned to follow Mendoza.

Chapter 3

January 1st Early morning

The music pounded all night in *Centro*—ricocheting off hotels, homes, and apartments until dawn. Throughout the night and into the early hours of the morning, families arrived, carrying ice chests with food and drinks, settling around reserved tables or spreading their party supplies on stone walls and public benches. Small children dressed in fancy clothes darted in and out among the tables and chairs. Even the three-year-olds kept time to the salsa beat. Eventually the pre-schoolers collapsed into any available space to nap fitfully until the party was over. Food and beer vendors lined the perimeter of the square, providing additional fuel for the dancers. The enticing smells of cooking food mingled with odors of perfume, sweat, and spent explosives.

By six in the morning the number of celebrants had dwindled to a few hundred. Sleepy children were packed up, along with remnants of the family feast. Yasmin surveyed the plaza in *Centro*. Discarded paper noisemakers, party hats, food wrappers, beer cans, and Coke bottles littered the square. *What a party!*

"Hey, Jessica, are you ready to head to Punta Sur?" Yasmin asked, hoping that her friend would change her mind and instead would want to go home to bed. Now that the dancing had stopped, she was tired, really tired. It was a good thing she had driven her *moto*, her little scooter, to the festivities. With this many people still milling around, finding a taxi was a big challenge. Finding a taxi driver who hadn't been celebrating with a few adult beverages was an even bigger challenge.

"Yep. First light is at six thirty-four," said Jessica, her sapphire-blue eyes glittering as she snatched up the last bottle of champagne and two glasses, stashed earlier in a disposable ice chest. Twenty-six years old, she was two years younger and two inches shorter than Yasmin, and her thick blond hair hung freely down to the middle of her back. Unlike her friend who rebuffed the idea of tattoos, Jessica's left arm was inked in a full sleeve, covered with whale sharks, turtles, and colorful tropical fish.

Checking the time on her phone, Yasmin said, "Tight, but we might make it." They walked rapidly to the scooter parked in an empty lot across the street from the church. Yasmin grinned as Jessica recklessly hitched her leg over the passenger seat, her short dress riding up over her slim thighs. *Good thing she wasn't commando today. That would have given the bystanders an eyeful.*

"All set, let's go," Jessica said.

Yasmin spun the moto around, driving in the wrong direction on Juarez Avenue, a one-way road behind the Navy base. The only traffic on the road was other celebrants either heading home or hurrying to greet the sunrise.

Weaving rapidly past a collection of slower vehicles, Yasmin and Jessica zipped along Aeropuerto Road, headed south. They bounced over the inescapable Mexican speed bumps, *topes,* at the gas station entrance, the school, and the kindergarten crosswalks, then turned left onto the perimeter road running along the eastern coastline. After negotiating over more bone-rattling speed bumps near the *Capilla de Guadalupe*—the beautiful chapel with stained-glass windows overlooking the azure sea—they had several minutes of *tope*-free driving to gain a little time.

At the turnoff road to the plaza at Punta Sur, red and blue lights strobing from the municipal police vehicles signalled the lane was closed. The parking lot was full; both sides of the street were jammed with vehicles. The patrolman waved Yasmin to the last parking spot available, placing the florescent orange cones behind her moto. The steady stream of traffic arriving seconds later was directed to park along both sides of the roadway.

Yasmin laughed, "We made it, with nine minutes to spare."

Still clutching the champagne bottle, Jessica hopped off the bike. "Don't forget the glasses," she said, pointing at the storage area under the seat.

There were cars, pickups, golf carts, motos, people, and pets. In the back of family trucks, mattresses and blankets had been added as makeshift beds, allowing tired children to nap. An enterprising food vendor was set up near the palapa, with a line of hungry patrons waiting for their tacos. Music blasted over the crowd from a nearby DJ. Every available space was crowded with bodies—the tops of the stone walls, the seats in the seldom-used amphitheater, the gardens, and the plaza. People were arriving with coolers of alcoholic beverages and open bottles of champagne.

Hundreds of people wandered the concrete path towards the ancient temple of the Goddess IxChel, heading for the crumbling stone stairway that wound down the cliff to the edge of the turquoise Caribbean Sea. Yasmin and Jessica were content to stay at the large star-fish shaped plaza at the top of the cliffs. It had a great view and didn't require hiking on the treacherous walkway in high heels. Jessica popped the champagne cork and poured a generous amount into both glasses.

Then the moment arrived, the first light of the year. "Happy New Year, my dear friend," said Jessica, holding up her champagne glass and clinking it against Yasmin's.

"And a very Happy New Year to you!" Yasmin replied, hugging Jessica while holding the brimming glass in her right hand. The rays of the rising sun reflected off the gold highlights in her curly dark hair, and her deep green eyes shone with happiness.

With a smile crinkling the corners of her eyes, Jessica leaned back so she could see Yasmin's expression. "So, what are we going to do with the sack of goodies that Sparky found yesterday?" she asked, referring to the small bag of what they hoped were Spanish doubloons, lost during their November treasure hunting fiasco.

Chapter 4

January 1st Sunrise

Carlos Mendoza groaned, pulling himself up onto one knee. He opened his eyes to sunlight and felt a blinding pain in his head. Scrunching his eyes shut, he reached to touch his head. His hands yanked to a stop just short of his skull. Bewildered, he looked down—he was handcuffed to a rusty metal pipe embedded in a rough concrete wall. His vision was blurry, and the back of his neck felt sticky. Shifting until he could touch his head, he gingerly explored the area, pulling back fingertips caked in dried blood.

Puzzled, he carefully rotated his head, checking his surroundings. *Where the hell am I?*

An empty building of some sort. No glass in the windows or doors covering the openings. The light breeze swirled dead leaves and bits of trash in the corners of the room. Smelly bird droppings were thickly spread over a cement counter. Moisture leaked from one wall, probably a cracked drain originally installed to remove the rainwater from the rooftop. Jerking on the shackles, he strained to rip the pipe away from the cement wall. No good. All that did was increase his dizziness and nausea.

14

He settled onto his haunches, trying to conserve his energy while he mulled over his predicament. He remembered having a couple of drinks with Yasmin and Jessica at the New Year's Eve celebrations, then waving goodbye and walking to where he had parked the Porsche. Between heading to his car and waking up with a headache that he doubted even four tablets of extra-strength ibuprofen would cure, he had no memory of what had happened. Stifling a moan, he stiffly lowered himself to the floor with his back propped against the wall. Christ, his head hurt. He hoped he didn't have a concussion.

He glanced down at his clothes. He was still wearing what he had had on the night before, tan chinos, black linen shirt, and loafers, but his pants were torn and his shoes were badly scuffed, like he had been dragged across a rough surface. His stainless-steel Rolex watch wasn't on his left wrist, and he couldn't feel the wallet that was normally tucked into his right hip pocket. His new iPhone, the latest model, was also missing. *Maybe this was just a robbery.*

But why handcuff him to a drainpipe in an abandoned building, if all the guy wanted was money and valuables? Kidnapping? Possible, especially since he was a businessman, but typically the kidnappers took someone from larger cities and who had a family rich enough to pay the ransom. That wouldn't work in his case. His sixty-year-old *papa* only owned one small fishing boat, a panga. His parents lived in an unpretentious house set on a sliver of land bordering the Salinas Grande, the landlocked lake in the center of the island. It wasn't the poorest neighborhood on the island, but was by no means the richest either. Looking for more affordable property, his two brothers and one sister had moved away from Isla Mujeres to the colonial city of Valladolid, located on the mainland. They lived happy, ordinary lives with their partners and an assortment of offspring.

He had income from the *Loco Lobo,* but he didn't own the restaurant location on Hidalgo Avenue; he leased it on a long-term basis. The balance of his assets was tied up in his one indulgence, the Porsche, and his modest casa; added together they might be worth the equivalent of a hundred thousand American dollars on a good day. It didn't make sense. He just wasn't rich enough to hold for ransom. If worse came to worse, he could probably arrange for the car to be sold and the cash given to the kidnappers. It wasn't much, but something at least.

Carlos could hear the muted sounds of traffic passing the building, engines slowing and then speeding up. A *tope* maybe? Motorbikes and vehicles slowing down to negotiate the speed bump? Despite the stench of pigeon droppings from dozens of birds using the empty building for shelter, he could smell the briny-fish scent of the ocean. He could see the swaying top of a palm tree, so he thought he must be somewhere near water, but he wasn't certain if he was still on Isla Mujeres, or maybe somewhere in Cancun. He could be in any one of the nearby oceanfront communities— Cancun, Puerto Morelos, Punta Sam, or even Progreso.

What the hell had happened?

Examining the area more thoroughly, he mentally estimated the dimensions of the room. The metal drainpipe that he was handcuffed to was secured to a roughed-in countertop, which indicated that part of the space was designed for an efficiency kitchen. A flat expanse of concrete, probably intended as a patio for the future owners or guests to enjoy the view, extended out into space. The overall area was comparable in size to a comfortable apartment, so he was probably in an unfinished multi-unit building similar to a condominium or apartment hotel.

Okay, if he was still on Isla, then it could be the large condo project on Playa Media Luna, abandoned due to lack of finances following the American economic crash in 2008. But the sounds of traffic on the pavement ruled out that location—that property was bordered on the north by regrown vegetation, and by beachfront on the eastern side. Listening intently, he suspected the ocean was on what he thought might be the western side of the structure, and there seemed to be sound-deadening vegetation surrounding it. So maybe it was the unfinished and derelict seventy-five room luxury hotel, the *Unik*, situated closer to Garrafon Natural Reef Park. *If* he was still on Isla.

Thirsty, head throbbing, and desperately needing to take a leak, Carlos shifted on the floor, trying to make himself more comfortable. Ah well, nothing for it, he'd have to take a piss and hope that most of the liquid would run the other direction. Fumbling with the zipper on his pants, he was able to relieve himself without splashing too much on his feet and legs. And of course, the urine sat right there, close enough that he might accidentally lay in it if he fell asleep again.

Great, just freaking great.

Leaning back against the concrete wall, he unsuccessfully attempted to find a comfortable position. If this was someone's idea of a joke, they were in for a nasty surprise, a very nasty surprise, when he got free.

At least the staff could take care of the *Loco Lobo* for him until he got clear of this situation. And then he thought of Yasmin. He prayed she was safe.

Chapter 5

January 1st Noon

"Well, damn. Look at that," Jessica Sanderson muttered as she flipped through the internet news on her iPhone. Slightly hungover from the previous night's festivities, she intended to consume large amounts of water today, and only water. It was going to be a no-alcohol day. The best cure for a hangover was time, water and aspirin.

In the background she could hear the prattle of Latino voices from one of the hugely popular Mexican telenovelas, the bodice-rippers of television. The women were always stunningly beautiful and the men breathtakingly handsome. Most storylines were based around the Cinderella-premise that life was nothing without a man, marriage, and children. Jessica occasionally left the television on as a means to learn colloquial Spanish, or for the company of a human voice, but most times she preferred to listen to music on her iPhone.

Jessica was fortunate. Her house was a little larger than the neighborhood norm, with two small bedrooms, a kitchen-living area, and a bathroom big enough to swing a cat. The *casita* had a fenced backyard just large enough for a bistro-style table and two chairs. It was the perfect location to catch a cooling breeze in the evening.

She swiped her phone screen, pushing the icon for Yasmin's often called number.

As the phone purred in her ear, Jessica stared out of her kitchen window watching Sparky, her short-legged rescue mutt, repeatedly sniffing and marking his territory. Genetically part-terrier and part of every other dog that ever lived on the island, he liked to investigate the garden several times a day, searching for the iguana living under a pile of rocks at the back of the yard. It was a live and let-live relationship between the short dog and hefty iguana, neither one aggressive toward or afraid of the other. Sparky ignored the fruit and vegetables scraps that Jessica offered to the iguana. Not his style. The iguana, on the other hand, was more than willing to eat dog food whenever it had the opportunity.

Jessica refreshed a tiny bowl of water sitting near the kitchen tap while listening as Yasmin's number continued to ring unanswered. The water was necessary for her diminutive resident reptile, Geek the Gecko. Hearing her moving around in the kitchen, Geek made a loud *chuk-chuk-chuk*, his way of saying 'Good morning' from his refuge behind the refrigerator. The gecko's body was a soft translucent pink, and was about the size of her index finger. He resembled a gelatin-candy reptile available in the penny candies at the local corner stores; three for one peso. In the past when Geek was thirsty, he tried to catch a drip from the kitchen tap, often miscalculating and falling into the slippery-sided basin with no traction for his Velcro-like feet, and no means of escape. After several panicky rescue operations, she decided to give him an accessible water supply. In return he ate the household mosquitoes.

"Come on Yasmin, answer!" Jessica muttered into her phone as it buzzed for the sixth time in her ear. With her free hand, she pushed open the screen door for Sparky.

Inside, Sparky leaned against her leg until she got the hint and bent over and roughly scratched his thick curly fur. She smiled as the dog's expression turned to one of pure bliss. The one part of his body that his stubby legs couldn't reach for a good scratch was right there, at the base of his spine.

"Bueno," came Yasmin's sleepy, and commonly used, island-style greeting.

"Yasmin, it's me." Jessica propped the phone under her chin while she filled Sparky's food bowl with a mix of cooked chicken, sweet potato, and vegetables. Setting the dish on the floor, she smiled at his cautious sniffing before he decided it was fit to eat.

"Hi, Jess," Yasmin said, yawning into her phone. "It seems like I just got to sleep." She stifled another yawn, "What's up?"

"I know it's only been a few hours, Yassy, but I just had to tell you." No matter what time they finally got to bed, Jessica always woke up earlier than Yasmin. "I have good news. Kirk Patterson is dead," Jessica blurted.

"What! How?"

Listening, Jessica could hear Yasmin moving around, probably sitting up in bed. It was an odd and very human trait how most people who answered the phone while laying down automatically either sat up or stood up, in an effort to better comprehend the conversation, to be more attentive.

21

"According to the news report dated four days ago," Jessica said, "the Sheriff's Department was transferring him from the county lockup, where he'd been held since mid-November, to a state prison to wait for his murder trial. The transport van was involved in a fatal crash."

Unseen by Jessica, Yasmin joyfully pumped her fist in the air. "Kirk Patterson's dead! Oh my god, that is such a relief." She self-consciously fingered a scar, a memento of when Patterson had pressed a razor-sharp switchblade under her chin, threatening to slice her throat.

Six weeks earlier, their lives had been turned upside down when she and Jessica, with help from Sparky, had discovered a huge cache of ancient treasure. The loot, taken in an attack on Veracruz in 1683, had been buried on Isla Mujeres by Captain Lorencillo de Graff then found and reburied by the pirate Fermin Mundaca.

The women had been in the process of digging up a few coins when Patterson grabbed Yasmin and held a knife to her throat, demanding they give him what they had found. As tropical storm Ricardo raged overhead, bringing torrential rain and high winds, Kirk had disappeared into the jungle with the handful of items secured in a small cloth sack. Then a few weeks later, there were news reports from Florida about his arrest on charges of rape and first-degree murder. He did not have the sack of loot with him when he was arrested.

Legally all of the valuables belonged to the Mexican government, and when the Instituto Nacional de Antropología e Historia (National Institute of Anthropology and History) team excavated the find, they uncovered a large hoard of gold doubloons, heavy gold artifacts, ornate jewelry, and numerous loose gems taken during the raid on Veracruz in 1683.

Curious about the size of the excavation, and hoping to start the year off on a healthier routine, Yasmin and Jessica had gone for a walk in the Hacienda Mundaca Park the previous morning. Jessica's dog, Sparky, had located the misplaced bag, which by the feel of it still contained a few coins and gems. Surprised at their good fortune, the two women had spirited the booty out of the park, hiding it in a slim laptop safe at Yasmin's.

At least the mystery of what had happened to the treasure that Patterson had snatched from them was solved. Yasmin hadn't told anyone, not even Carlos, about their recent discovery. She and Jessica hadn't had time to figure out what to do.

Yasmin nodded her head as she listened to Jessica re-read the entire article to her over the phone. "That's awesome news about Patterson," she said when Jessica stopped reading. "Absolutely awesome. I am going to phone Mom and Dad and tell them the good news."

At the other end of the conversation Jessica chuckled, "You think that will stop her from worrying about her baby daughter? Not likely."

"True," Yasmin agreed with a light laugh. "I'll see you later at work," she said, ending the call.

Since she was awake, Yasmin decided she might as well call her parents now. They, as well as her older sister Adriana and family, lived a few hours away on the Yucatan peninsula in the beautiful city of Mérida. Yasmin's mother, the formidable Maria Victoria Guzman de Medina, insisted she was to be called 'Victoria,' correctly pronounced in Spanish as *Bic-tor-ia*. From an early age she had refused to use her first name, as many of her friends were also named Maria in honor of the Virgin Mary, as was her mother-in-law, Maria Medina. Too many women with the same first name had prompted Victoria to give her daughters the less common names of Adriana and Yasmin.

Yasmin flipped the covers aside and put her feet on the floor, padding towards the kitchen to start the coffee. She needed coffee, lots of coffee, before chatting with her mom.

Chapter 6

January 1st Mid-day

"Hey, tough guy. Wake up." A foot sharply booted Carlos in the ribs as he lay dozing on the floor of the abandoned building. "Not so scary now, are you?" the voice taunted.

"You!" Carlos grunted in pain and surprise. He hadn't heard the person approaching, "I thought you were in jail, in Florida." His headache was fierce, making coherent thoughts difficult.

"Thanks to you and your two thugs, I was." Kirk Patterson, or Kyle Johnson, depending on what name he was currently using, was thinner than the last time Carlos had seen him; his head was shaved, and he had grown a beard. Still, the cold blue eyes were the same, vacant and soulless. Patterson smirked, "By the way, thank you for the nice ride on that pretty boat. What's the name of it? Oh yeah, the *Sea Bitch*," he grinned sarcastically. "Can't say your buddies are very good hosts though, leaving me trussed up like a turkey for sixteen hours."

"*Sea Witch*, and it was better treatment than you deserved." Carlos tensed his stomach muscles as the second kick landed on the same rib. He felt the rib give a little, and sharp pain radiated through his chest. Likely cracked if not broken. "I should have told them to feed you to the sharks instead of delivering you to the Sheriff's Department in Florida," Carlos quietly gasped out the words between shallow breaths. He wasn't going to show the son of a bitch how badly he was hurt.

"I'll be sure to thank them when I pay them a visit."

Carlos lightly shrugged his shoulders. His friends, Diego Avalos and his brother-in-law Pedro Velazquez, were strong, capable guys. The three of them had been buddies since they were pre-schoolers, and had remained fast friends all through their lives. By the time they had graduated from *Secundaria Técnica* at the ages of fifteen and sixteen, they were edging towards petty crimes. Fortunately for them, Pedro's uncle Manolo had realized what was happening and had administered a few well-placed slaps to the head, and a rough 'get-your-shit-together and don't-be-a-*pendejo*' speech. The guys could take care of themselves. Right now, Carlos had other more pressing concerns.

"How did you get me here?" he probed, still fuzzy on what had happened.

"Simple. You were busy unlocking your car, so I gave you a little love tap on the back of your head with a baseball bat, then stuffed you in your own car." Leaning against an unfinished counter, Patterson casually crossed one leg over the other, a smug expression on his face. "I drove you here and dragged your sorry ass up the stairs to the third floor."

Carlos grunted disparagingly, "I'm well-known on Isla. Someone probably saw you and reported the incident to my friends or to the policía."

"Don't get your hopes up. Everyone was busy getting drunk for New Year's Eve. No one was paying any attention." Kirk pressed against the counter, his fingertips shoved into his pockets, grinning down at Carlos. "Nice car by the way. I left it outside your house all safe and sound, although you won't be driving it again. Your family can argue over who gets to keep it."

"How did you get away? Last we heard you were being held for a murder trial." Carlos could feel his eyelids drooping as he struggled to stay alert. He was exhausted, in pain, and had a raging thirst.

One side of his mouth twitching up in a smirk, Kirk said, "The gods were smiling on me a few days ago. The sheriffs were transporting me north to a State Penitentiary, and their van was involved in a crash, rear-ended by a trucker transporting a big sport-fishing boat. The force of the collision popped open the rear door of the van and crumpled the driver's compartment, trapping the two deputies inside. I was able to scramble my way out. Luckily I found a few gallons of gas in the back of the transport rig."

Carlos scrunched his eyebrows together. What Patterson had just said wasn't making any sense. "Gasoline? So what, you temporarily escaped. But they know you are still alive and the US and Mexico have an extradition agreement."

"Nope. I'm dead. The television reports say I perished in the vehicle fire along with the two deputies. Poor unfortunate me." His mouth stretched in a grin that didn't reach his eyes, "However, the truck driver is missing and being sought on a country-wide warrant for leaving the scene of a fatal accident. The inferno incinerated the bodies, and is making positive identification difficult."

Carlos glared at Patterson, thinking how much he would like to get his hands around the other man's throat to finish this once and for all. His previous decision, to spirit Patterson back to Florida and hand him over to the Sheriff's Department, was obviously the wrong one. It was now coming back to bite him in the ass, hard. He should have just killed him the first time.

"How did you get back into Mexico?" Carlos asked. Right now, he was at a huge disadvantage, but maybe, just maybe, if he kept asking Patterson questions, his overtired brain could figure out an escape plan.

"Easy. The same method your buddies used to take me to Florida. I hopped on a private sport-fishing boat that was headed from Texas to Isla for the sailfish season. Helped out as a deck hand until we docked. I then just disappeared over the side before the customs official arrived."

Clapping his hands together, Patterson smirked, "Well, I'd love to stay and chat, but I've got stuff to do today. I want to spend a little quality time with your pretty girlfriend, Yasmin. We have unfinished business."

Kicking out at Patterson, Carlos raged, "Leave Yasmin out of this. If you have a problem with me, then let's deal with it. Release me and we'll settle this here and now."

"Release you? What? You think I want a fair fight?" Patterson laughed, then pointed at a gallon jug on the floor, "I left you water. I don't want you dying too soon. I have plans to entertain you while your little girlfriend and I get to know each other better."

Patterson pointed a cellphone at Carlos and snapped a photo, "Smile." He glanced at the photo, checking that the image was sharp, then added, "Yasmin will enjoy seeing this. See ya later, loser."

Furious, Carlos yanked on his handcuffs as he watched Patterson disappear into the vacant building. His sudden forceful movements intensified the pain in his ribs and made him nauseated from the whack on the head. *How the hell am I going to get free?*

Chapter 7

January 1st Late afternoon

Yasmin smoothly pulled her *Italika* motor scooter into a slot where most of the Hidalgo Avenue restaurant and bar employees parked their motos. Even though it had been purchased almost two months before, she kept it clean and new looking. The *moto* was her baby.

She set the kickstand to support the bike and stepped off. Unbuckling her helmet, she pulled it from her head, finger fluffing her dark, blond-streaked hair. She lifted the seat on the moto and placed the helmet in the under-seat storage compartment. A quick flick of the key and everything was secure.

Threading through the crowds on Hidalgo Avenue, Yasmin noticed a high percentage of people looked a little worse for wear after the all-night celebrations. Some appeared to have continued partying, still wearing their dressy clothes from the night before, and by now they were getting their second wind, ready to carry on for a few more hours. The real hangovers would start tomorrow, when the effects of no sleep and too much alcohol finally caught up with the revelers.

The same scene would repeat itself in a month or so during *Carnaval* when the Saturday night fiesta, complete with more fireworks and another big band, would celebrate again until dawn. The only difference being people didn't drive to Punta Sur to greet the dawn after *Carnaval*. Revelers usually went home to bed for a few hours before resuming the celebrations during the Sunday afternoon parade of the dance troupes.

At times like this Yasmin was thankful she lived in the colonias, away from the hectic atmosphere in *Centro*. She liked her eight hours of sleep, burrowed under the covers with the room-darkening curtains pulled tightly closed. Her neighborhood in the colonias wasn't always the quietest location, but she had learned as an infant that to survive in a Mexican culture you had to be able to tune out the noise.

Early rising roosters greeted the new day an hour before sunrise. Dogs, common in all homes except hers it seemed, barked when other canines crossed their territory, or when a motorcycle passed by, or at nothing at all. In the cool of the evening, when one mutt began to howl, others nearby would join in the chorus. The noise would spread through the *colonia* until the beasts were bored with the tune.

During the daylight hours, the grackles, large black crow-like birds, screeched and fought over scraps of food. Groups of young teenagers giggled and chatted late into the night, conveniently forgetting that school commenced at seven in the morning. Singing, or sometimes arguing, adults added to the tumult. The gunshot-like sounds of backfiring motos, the clatter of golf carts driven by locals as their primary mode of transportation, and the grumble of big trucks were commonplace. Loud music played into the early hours of the morning.

Her culture was a noisy vivacious society, vastly different from the one that Jessica described when talking about her home town in Canada where regulations forbade excessive noise after eleven in the evening. That was hard to imagine.

Swinging her bag over her shoulder, she strode towards Carlos' restaurant, the *Loco Lobo*, where she and Jessica worked. It was a pleasantly warm afternoon in the middle of the winter dry season, with very little rain, and low humidity. It was a perfect temperature for her skinny jeans and a silky top.

Every few weeks during the winter months, a *Norte*, a storm from the north, would arrive, bringing cooler temperatures and winds from the chillier climates of the USA and Canada. Much to the amusement of visiting northerners who seldom wore anything other than shorts and tops, the island residents keenly felt the ten degrees drop in temperature. Parents bundled children in padded jackets and woolen sweaters, then pulled knitted caps over their heads. In some cases, the state government would issue health warnings when the temperatures dropped to sixteen degrees Celsius, or as Carlos said, sixty-one degrees American. Usually after three or four days, a high-pressure system coming out of the southern Atlantic Ocean would reassert itself and the island would be back to sunny t-shirt and shorts weather.

The *Loco Lobo* was a popular location on the island, serving good food and generous drinks. The background music was a fun mix of current tunes in English and Spanish. The shady and cool interior had black granite counter tops, stamped concrete floors and navy and lime green upholstery. Large framed pictures taken by a well-known local photographer and tour boat captain, Tony Garcia, adorned three walls. Depicting the simpler side of island life, his photos included colorful open-deck *panga* fishing boats, the fishermen repairing their nets on the beach, or old islanders with faces weathered by time and hard work. The fourth wall wasn't really a wall, but an intricate metal security gate that rolled up and out of the way, allowing the restaurant to spill out into Hidalgo Avenue with additional tables and chairs.

Happy with life and relieved that any lingering danger of Kirk Patterson had passed, Yasmin smiled at friends and acquaintances as she sauntered into the busy restaurant. Jessica waved from the other side where she was taking orders for a group of exuberant tourists.

From behind the bar, Isabela called out, "Yasmin, I am so glad to see you!" Having recently been promoted from night-time assistant to the day-time bartender, Isabela was rapidly arranging drinks for a large order. "We are really swamped with customers today."

"Hola, Isabela," Yasmin responded and quickly pecked her friend on the cheek. Then she turned and did a quick visual check around the packed restaurant. "Full house. Give me five minutes to get myself organized."

"Sure, no problem."

"Is Carlos in?" Yasmin asked, quickly stashing her purse in the staff storage area.

Isabela paused momentarily and looked at Yasmin with a puzzled frown. "No, now that you mention it, I haven't seen him at all," she said, as she swiftly resumed working on the drink orders. "That's very odd. He's usually here super early on New Year's Day. It's one of our busiest times of the year."

Slipping the bartender's apron over her clothes, Yasmin doubled the apron strings around her slim waist and tied them into a neat bow. "That's really strange. Last night he left the fiesta just after the midnight fireworks. He planned to open early this morning for the all-night party crowd."

Perplexed, Yasmin checked her phone again, hoping he had called while she was driving to work. *Nothing. Where are you Carlos?* She dropped the phone into her pocket, and washed her hands. "Okay, what have you got going on here with this crowd?"

Both women worked rapidly, pouring drinks and Isla Brewing micro-brewed draft ales. Isabela stayed an hour past her shift to help clear the backlog of orders. Finally, by five in the afternoon, the crowds were thinning as people wandered away to nap for a few hours before resuming the festivities.

Yasmin restlessly checked her phone. Still nothing from Carlos. "Damn it, I wonder where he is. I had some good news that I wanted to share with him," she muttered softly, unaware that she had spoken out loud.

"Good news?" Isabela cocked an eyebrow at Yasmin. "Care to share with me?" she asked, as she undid her bartender's apron and wearily hung it in the staff room.

"Sure, I'm busting to tell someone," Yasmin said with a quick nod of acknowledgement. "Remember last November when Jessica and I got into a bit of a predicament?" she said.

"Predicament?" Isabela laughed, "That's understating it just a bit, don't you think? That was the mother lode of Spanish loot. The reporters hounded you and Jessica for weeks. You were famous." Isabela leaned back on the counter, grinning. "So, did you get to keep anything?"

Blushing, Yasmin glanced away, "Er, no. We had always intended to turn over whatever we had found. We just sort of got carried away in the excitement of the discovery." She wiped the granite counter top, avoiding eye contact with her work mate.

"Okay, so what's the good news then?"

"Well," Yasmin turned to look at Isabela, "Jessica just noticed an internet report about Kirk Patterson, the guy that attacked me. He died in a vehicle accident a few days ago while being transferred from a county jail to a state prison. It's a big relief for me."

"That is good news. I can see that would make you feel better." Isabela gave Yasmin a quick hug, then signed out for the day. "When you see that lazy boss of ours, tell him I said 'Hi.' Take care, see you tomorrow."

"Adios, Isabela," Yasmin waved, then turned to quickly restock her bar supplies, readying for the next onslaught.

"Hey you. How are you? This is the first time I've been able to take a breather," Jessica said as she bustled over to the bar with a lengthy order for a table of eight customers.

"Great news about Kirk!" She raised a hand in a high-five gesture, and Yasmin happily slapped palms with her.

"It's awesome news. I am so relieved."

"Me too, but right now I need six frozen margs with salt, and two glasses of Sauv Blanc," Jessica rattled off the server-shorthand for her drink orders.

"Have you seen Carlos?" Yasmin asked, as she deftly organized the drinks onto Jessica's serving tray.

"Nope. Strange. He's normally here at shift change, to give us our daily pep-talk, our marching orders," Jessica said, then continued, "he probably had an appointment or decided to take a few hours off."

"Isabela hasn't seen him all day."

Jessica stopped momentarily, considering the information, "Definitely not normal for him. Why don't you ring his cell number?" She swung her heavy tray up near her right shoulder, allowing her right arm to take most of the weight while her left arm steadied it.

"I keep checking for messages from him. The last thing he said to me before he left the party last night was that he was going to be here early to feed the hungry drunks. He wouldn't take the day off, especially not today."

"Just phone him." Jessica said as she stepped away.

Chapter 8

January 1st Late afternoon

Jessica rested her empty tray on the bar counter, listening as Yasmin finished her message for Carlos.

"Hola, *mi amor*. I'm just checking to see if everything is okay. We missed you today," Yasmin said, before disconnecting.

Jessica asked, "Any luck finding him?"

"No answer, it just goes to voice mail. I hope he's alright."

"I'm sure he's fine. But, just in case, I'll call Diego and see if he knows anything." Jessica pulled her phone out of its storage location, pushed into the side of her bra. It was a convenient place to keep it, it didn't create an unsightly bulge in the pocket of her shorts, and she could feel the vibrate mode if someone phoned her while she was working. She pushed the icon for Diego's cell, listening until she heard his familiar voice, "*Hola*, handsome. How are you?"

"*Bien, mi bella*." His rich laugh sounded in her ear. "Maybe a little headache from too much tequila last night, but I'll survive. And you?"

"I'm good. Tired, but okay. Thanks," she said, turning to check that her customers were content while she talked to Diego. "Do you or Pedro know where Carlos is?"

"I have no idea," Diego said. "Did you ask Yasmin if she knows where he is?"

"Yes, she is the one that mentioned that no one has seen or heard from him today. We're getting a bit worried."

"And she called his cell?"

"Yep, it goes straight to voice mail."

Jessica could hear Diego talking to his brother-in-law and business partner, Pedro, asking if he knew where Carlos might be. "Jessica, Pedro hasn't heard from him either. We're just finishing up with a sailfish charter and should be back at the docks in thirty minutes. As soon as our clients are ashore, we'll head over to his place and check on him, okay?"

"Is that thirty minutes gringo-time or Mexican-time?" she teased, referring to the cultural habit of quoting a time and showing up anywhere from one to three hours late. Invitations to birthday parties that clearly stated the party started at three in the afternoon, in fact meant the hosts would be decorating around three, showering and getting dressed for the festivities around four, and perhaps ready for guests around five. It wasn't considered rude to be late, or even very late. Time was relative, you got there when you got there, and stayed longer because, well, you were late getting there.

"Ha, we'll be back in thirty minutes."

"Okay, if we hear from him or see him before then, I'll let you know."

"*Claro, gracias amiga.*"

"*Adios*, sweet-cheeks," she added with a flirt in her voice. Diego was happily married with four young children and a beautiful wife, Cristina, whom he adored. The two friends had an unspoken understanding; her flirting was just harmless fun.

Ending the conversation, Jessica turned to Yasmin. "You probably heard. Diego doesn't know where Carlos is either. He and Pedro are out on one of those sailfish photography charters that they do. He'll check once they get back to the island."

"I'm sure he's fine, but it's just so out-of-character for him not to let anyone know that he wasn't coming in today." Yasmin's attention was drawn by an increase in the noise level of the restaurant. "Heads up, look at that big group." Her hands busy with assembling a drink order, Yasmin pointed her chin towards the tables and chairs set up on the street. Twenty or more boisterous people looked like they were settling in for an evening of fun.

"On it!" Jessica scooted over to the table, flashing the stunning result of five years of teenage braces and endless orthodontist visits. "Hi guys, where are you from?"

A chorus of replies came back; Ontario, California, Oregon, Arizona, British Columbia, Wisconsin, and Indiana.

"And what brings you to our little paradise?"

A tall red-head smiled at an equally tall man to her right, "We're getting married in two days. These are our friends who have come to Isla for our wedding."

"Congratulations!" Jessica said, "I'm sure you will have a fabulous wedding and fall in love with our island. Now, first drinks then food," Jessica rested her tray on one hip, individually making eye contact with each person. "We're famous for our frozen margaritas, mojitos, and our local microbrewery's draft ales. We can make most any type of mixed drink, and we have wine plus the regular brands of beer."

"Margs! Jugs of margs!"

"A mojito."

"Wine for me please, white wine."

"I'll take a draft pale ale."

Laughing, Jessica held up a hand, "Let's try that again, one order at a time, please." She pointed her pen at the redhead, "The bride-to-be, what is your name?"

"Sarah," she replied.

"Okay, Sarah, let's start with you, since you are the guest of honor this weekend."

"I'll have a glass of white wine, please, no margaritas for me until after the wedding." She turned and smiled at her mate, "Steve and I both know what happens when I drink margs." The man she referred to as Steve just grinned and winked.

Around eight in the evening, a sour-looking woman plunked herself down at a table for two, frowning as she searched the room for a server. At a quick glance, Jessica estimated the woman was in her mid-forties, a little pudgy around the middle, and dressed in clothes that would probably look better on a woman twice her age. Jessica did a quick look to see who was available, but the other servers were occupied running food and drinks to customers. She made eye contact with the new arrival and held up an index finger to indicate she would be there in a minute or two, as soon as she finished closing out the bills for the wedding party table. The group had stayed for three hours, eating, drinking, and laughing at their inside jokes.

"Best wishes for your wedding!" Jessica said, briefly hugging the bride and groom. "I hope to see you again before you leave the island."

"Thanks Jessica," Sarah replied, "this was so much fun, we'll definitely be back."

Turning to greet her new customer, Jessica handed an open menu to the woman. "Welcome to the *Loco Lobo*. May I get you a drink to start?"

The woman turned her unsmiling gaze to Jessica, "Is service always this slow here?"

"I'm so sorry you had to wait a few minutes. This is our busiest day of the year." A happy-server smile plastered on her face, Jessica looked at the woman. *Seriously? Slow service?*

"I'll have a glass of white wine. And make sure it is cold. I hate warm wine."

"Certainly, anything else? Something to eat perhaps?"

"Is your kitchen clean?"

"Yes, of course. We have regular health inspections."

"I'll think about it," she said, as she laid the unread menu on the table.

Fortunately, Jessica was able to scoot behind the bar and pour the glass of wine herself. Nodding with her head towards the single woman, she explained to Yasmin, "Sorry to invade your space Yassy, but that one is a bit picky. I didn't want to make her wait." She added with a light snicker, "Apparently she hates warm wine."

Yasmin grinned and nodded, too busy to chat.

"And here you go," Jessica said placing the glass of wine on the table. "Now, any decision on food?"

The woman glared at Jessica, "What are your bathrooms like?"

Nonplussed, Jessica repeated, "Bathrooms? I'm not sure what you mean?" *What the hell? Does she think she'll get diarrhea from our food?*

"Do you insist your guests throw used toilet paper in the garbage can? That is such a filthy and disgusting practice. Or can I just flush it?"

Jessica tamped down her grin, realizing that new visitors to Isla, and for that matter most of Mexico, didn't understand the reason for not flushing toilet paper. In many old towns and cities there were no sewer systems. Everything went into holding tanks that had to be pumped out on a regular basis. And the pumper trucks, that was another stinky problem, squeezing into the narrow streets to access the tanks. There was nothing remotely nice about a visit from the *Agua Negra* pumper. At least *Centro* had waste removal pipes, but the pumps that moved everything along to the sewerage plant near the southern end of the island occasionally malfunctioned, and then things got interesting, really interesting.

Smiling politely at the woman, Jessica answered, "Well, we do ask that you place the toilet paper in the covered container provided." She was certain that her reply would erase any chance of a tip. Most visitors understood the reason, apparently not this woman.

"Disgusting!" the woman sputtered.

"Yes, but..." Jessica started to explain, but the woman cut her off.

"I thought it was just that awful hotel where I am staying that does that. You know, that one on the other side of the square. That hotel has a top rating, but I think it's a dump. No elevator. No one to carry your bags for you. Small rooms. Two small pools. A small and very greasy breakfast."

Wanting to see the back of this woman as soon as possible, tip or no tip, Jessica's face relaxed into her public smile. She nodded her head in understanding letting the woman continue her seemingly unstoppable tirade.

"And no televisions. I couldn't watch CNN news. Who ever heard of such a thing—no televisions? It's a dump. I posted my no-star review on Trip Advisor," the woman said, as she nodded her head in self-congratulations.

"Yes, I see your problem," Jessica's lips twitched as she clamped down on a wise-ass retort. She knew exactly which top rated boutique hotel with the best repeat clientele and fabulous breakfasts the woman was criticizing. "Perhaps an all-inclusive on the Maya Riviera would be a more satisfying choice for you," she sweetly suggested, as she rolled her eyes behind the woman's back.

Chapter 9

January 1st Sundown

The twin twelve-hundred-horse engines on the fifty-eight-foot Viking, the *Bruja del Mar*, purred quietly as Pedro Velazquez expertly backed the boat into her berth at the Club de Yates Marina, locally known as the Lima docks or sometimes the Bally Hoo wharf. Located just off Rueda Medina, the main road that ran along the western side of the island, the docks were home-base to most of the high-end charter boats. Historically one of the oldest wharfs on the island, the facilities, including the Bally Hoo Restaurant and marine gas station, were owned by the Lima family, one of the original island dynasties. It was a convenient location, close to the highest concentration of the better hotels and their affluent customers.

Diego Avalos leapt onto the wharf and did a quick wrap of the lines, securing the stern and port side of the boat. Taller than the average Mayan man, Diego moved with the muscular grace of someone accustomed to physical work. His often-broken nose gave him a slightly menacing presence, which at times in his turbulent past had been useful. His dark-chocolate-colored eyes were warm and friendly as he grasped the forearm of a client, steadying the man as he stepped from the boat to the wharf.

Photography charters were his favorite type of business. No muss, no fuss. Just happy folks toting expensive underwater cameras with a sack full of accessories, who wanted to swim with the sailfish, swordfish, and marlin and make beautiful videos. It was a great sideline to their normal catch'em and eat'em charters where the customers reeled in tasty tuna, wahoo, or dorado. Back at the docks, the fish suitable for grilling would be cleaned and divided between the fishermen, who typically arranged with the manager of Bally Hoo to cook their catch for an evening meal. If a customer did want to fish for the sailfish, it was only on a catch and release basis.

With the photography-only charters, all they had to worry about was overly enthusiastic middle-aged guys getting poked in the ass by the rapier-sharp bill of a sailfish. In the frenzy of the hunt, the predators powered through the water, swarming the naturally occurring bait balls. Hunting inside a panicked shape-shifting blob, containing thousands of palm-sized sardines, the big fish struck again and again, until they were satiated. The clients were usually absorbed by the fascinating view through the camera lens, not watching their rear ends. Getting between a sailfish and its food was a fool-hardy act. Knock on wood, in the six years they had been offering this type of experience they hadn't had any injuries. And the money was much better than a standard charter.

"Amazing experience guys," a pale-skinned, rotund man boomed, "and what a bonus to see wild dolphins and sea turtles. I'll be passing on your contact information to my friends and business associates." The group gathered up the cameras, housing units, extra lenses, and lights, then carefully tucked the expensive equipment into fitted foam cradles inside waterproof bags.

"Awesome job," another client said as he shook Diego's hand, leaving him a hundred-dollar bill as a tip. "I've got some incredible shots of the sailfish attacking the sardines. And those huge frigate birds, diving into the bait balls when they broke the surface. Fabulous!" Smiling, the client turned to Pedro, who had joined them on the dock, shaking his hand and offering the same healthy gratuity in addition to what they had already been paid for the all-day charter for the ten men.

"Thank you, see you next time." Handshakes all around—several of which included a folded twenty- or fifty-dollar bill—and the group moved into the Bally Hoo eatery at the head of the dock to relive their adventure over drinks and dinner.

Smiling as he pocketed the money, Pedro murmured an aside to his brother-in-law, "Nice guys."

"Yep, and nice tips." Diego had already tucked the bills into the front pocket of his comfortable Hook & Tackle fishing shorts. "As soon as we get finished here, I promised Yasmin and Jessica we'd check on Carlos. They haven't heard from him today, he's not answering his phone, and they are worried about him."

"Okay, no problem. Let's secure the boat; we can come back and finish the cleanup chores later," Pedro said, as he skilfully tied bumpers between the finger-wharf and the boat, his shaved head gleaming in the setting sun.

Shorter than his brother-in-law, Pedro had the broad shoulders, long torso, and sturdy legs of his Mayan ancestors. His deep-set brown eyes and blade-shaped nose were reminiscent of the carvings on the ancient pyramids of Chichen Itza.

Diego fastened the bow and an additional spring line, then turned to Pedro, who was headed into the main salon of the boat. "Can you grab my go-bag when you lock up?"

"Got it," Pedro said as he turned the key in the lock. "Okay, let's go see what's up with Carlos."

"Stupid bugger probably forgot to tell his staff that he was taking a day off." Diego started his Jeep, and turning his head to look over his shoulder, backed it out of the cramped customers' only parking area in front of the Bally Hoo Restaurant. He checked for oncoming vehicles and smoothly pulled out into the traffic on Rueda Medina, flicking on the Jeep's headlights.

"Maybe," Pedro said, agreeably, "but why wouldn't he be answering his cell?"

"Good point. He usually keeps in touch with the employees even if he isn't at the restaurant." Diego's gaze swept over the palm trees in the center median. They would remain decorated with Christmas-themed displays and spiraling strands of rope lighting until the middle of January, well after the Día de Reyes, Three Kings' Day, a Catholic celebration more important than Christmas in Latin America.

"And Yasmin too. The guy is in serious lust over her."

"No kidding," Diego chuckled, "head-over-dick in lust with her."

Sitting on a bench in front of the taxi stand was a familiar young man, the stumps of his legs dangling above the ground; a set of crutches leaned against the bench. Both of his feet had been amputated a while back, a complication of unchecked diabetes.

Diego exhaled noisily and pulled the vehicle to the curb. Extending a fifty-peso note to Pedro, he said, "Can you give that to William?"

"Sure," Pedro leaned out far enough to reach the man's outstretched hand. "*Felicidades*, William," he said, a smile in his voice as he handed him the pesos.

"Gracias, muchas gracias," the man said with a thankful nod of his head.

"De nada," Pedro replied politely and waved goodbye.

"Poor guy," Diego muttered, "The diabetes problem in Mexico is a damn disgrace."

"Si. My friend Karen likes to help out at the free clinic on the island. She said the number of islanders, especially seniors, who have undiagnosed symptoms is alarming."

"I badger my parents to get checked every year. Pretty soon it will be my kids pestering me, their old dad," Diego said, thinking about how quickly time passed and how each day his four youngsters seemed a little older, a little more mature. *Can't slow down time*, he thought, deciding to talk about something more cheerful.

"Only six more weeks and Carnaval starts."

Pedro turned his head slightly towards Diego and asked, "How's my sister doing with her dance routines?"

"Good, really good. Cristina loves that stuff," Diego smiled, thinking about his wife modeling the sexy dance costumes created for the annual event. "This year she's all done up in blue, and yellow, and green. Lots of feathers, and sequins, and beads. She's a magnificent looking woman."

"She's my little sister—of course she's gorgeous," Pedro said. "It's in our genes."

"She is gorgeous. The only thing in your 'jeans' is your ugly butt," Diego snorted a laugh, grinning at his brother-in-law.

The sun had disappeared for the night, sinking rapidly below the horizon, by the time they were at Carlos' house. Diego pointed at the crookedly parked Porsche. "Not like him to make a mess of parking his baby."

"Curiouser, and curiouser." Frowning at the strangely parked car, Pedro checked for obstructions on the constricted sidewalk before flinging the passenger door on the Jeep open. His wide and well-muscled physique didn't slide gracefully through a half-opened car door, he needed it fully extended.

"Curious-what?" Diego asked over his shoulder, as he approached the front entrance.

"It's a quote from *Alice In Wonderland*."

"Uh huh, whatever." Diego raised his hand and knocked on the yellow wooden door. The enamel was so glossy the street light shining over his shoulder reflected his image in the paint.

"Carlos? Hey man, you okay?" Diego's big and calloused fist banged on the wood again. "Carlos? Are you home?" Silence greeted his thumping. Bending down, he lifted a conch shell lying beside the front steps. Singing a line from his favorite Kenny Chesney tune, he said, "The key's in the conch shell, come on in."

"Seriously? He's still doing the key under the shell thing?"

"Yep, he doesn't worry too much about theft. Only a total knucklehead would steal from him, and the other wanna-be gangstas would rat out the knucklehead to gain cred with Carlos." Diego inserted the key, turned the handle, and opened the door halfway. "Carlos? You home?"

Chapter 10

January 1st Late evening

Diego's shout went unanswered. He pulled his carbon-fiber ZT fishing knife from his front pocket and locked it in the open position.

The knife had a wicked looking four-and-a-half-inch blade that glinted in the light from the street lamp. For fishermen, a knife could be the difference between life and death when dealing with big, angry sea critters. Many of their friends had been seriously injured by the large slashing teeth of the barracudas or wahoo fighting for their lives as they were reeled onto the boat. Most island men habitually carried a sharp blade for emergencies.

With his left hand, Diego swept the door wide open, while the hand holding the knife reached for a wall switch. A soft click and the hallway was bathed in light.

"Hey bud, are you in?" Diego asked, cautiously walking further into the one-level, compact dwelling, keeping his back to the walls wherever possible, and flicking on lights as he moved from room to room. Diego flipped on the light in the only bedroom, raising his voice a little so that Pedro could hear, "His bed is made and the towels in the bathroom are dry. It doesn't look like he slept here last night."

"I don't think he's been home recently. No coffee cup in the sink. No beer bottles in the trash," Pedro said, his eyes roving from side to side as he searched the kitchen area, gripping his folding knife.

"But his car is here," Diego reminded Pedro. He turned his head slightly to speak over his shoulder while keeping his concentration on his search. "Check the closets and storage areas. I'll look in the yard."

Using the flashlight mode of his smartphone, Diego swept the light across the back patio, then walked the perimeter of the small yard, stooping to look under flowering hibiscus bushes and checking behind a plumeria tree. *Nothing*.

Fifteen minutes later, the two men stood in the kitchen, staring at each other as they mulled over the situation. "So, his car is here. He's not. And no one at the restaurant has seen him today." Diego propped his arms across his chest, his right hand stroking his chin while he thought. "Something is definitely not right."

"Got any other ideas?" Pedro closed his knife and stashed it in the right-hand pocket of his shorts.

"Call Yasmin again. Maybe she's heard from him but has been too busy to tell us."

Pedro tugged his phone out of his breast pocket, and swept an index finger across the screen, bringing the phone to life. He tapped the keys for Yasmin's number as he leaned back against the kitchen counter, relaxed but aware of his surroundings. When she answered on the third ring, he said, "Hola, Yasmin, this is Pedro."

"Did you find him?" she demanded, her voice loud and strident from a combination of stress and loud background noise.

"No, he's not at his house, but his car is. You still haven't heard from him?" He stuck an index finger in his left ear, trying to hear Yasmin over the din of the busy restaurant.

"No, nothing. I've phoned his number at least six times, but it goes straight to voice mail."

Glancing over at Diego, Pedro shook his head, negative. "Okay, try not to worry. Phone if you hear anything." Ending the call, Pedro studied the floor. "Okay," he said, tilting his worried gaze towards Diego, "let's check with a few of the guys, then we should stop by the hospital. Maybe, just maybe, he was hit by a drunk when he was walking to his car on New Year's Eve."

"Then how did his car end up parked outside his house?"

"I don't know, someone could have driven it there for him I guess."

A snort was Diego's immediate response, "Maybe, but everyone knows Carlos. We would have heard something by now."

"Maybe, maybe not. There are a lot of hungover people who could be sleeping off last night's party, and we were out on that photography charter all day. Maybe the news just hasn't got to us yet."

At the community hospital entrance, Diego bounded down the short flight of stairs, heading towards his Jeep. Frustrated, he flung open the unlocked driver's door and pulled himself behind the steering wheel. Their inquiries at the hospital had amounted to nothing. Lots of reports of injuries from drunken mishaps, and one domestic dispute, but no unidentified bodies, no vehicle accidents. Nothing.

Pedro settled into the passenger seat, lightly slapping the padded dash. "Damn it, where is that guy?" He flicked his phone on and once again called Yasmin. "Hola, Yassy."

"Any news?"

"No nothing," he replied, stifling a deep yawn. "Diego and I need to catch a few of hours of sleep. We've been up for over thirty hours and need to recharge our batteries."

"Si, yes of course. I understand," Yasmin quickly agreed, but Pedro could hear the distress in her voice.

"Yasmin, you know Carlos is a capable guy. He'll be fine."

"Yes, I know, but still, I'm really worried."

"Don't be. He'll be fine," Pedro said, his glance flicking sideways to Diego as he shrugged his shoulders. Perhaps he was exaggerating a little, but Yasmin needed to sleep as well or she wouldn't be much help tomorrow. "Are you and

Jessica okay to lock up the *Loco Lobo*? Or do you need a hand?" he asked, hoping she wouldn't ask them to come and help. Good Christ, he was tired. Too much tequila, beer, and dancing the night before, then an all-day boat charter with the group of Americans. Sleep. He needed at least eight hours of sleep.

"We'll be fine. We have both locked up before so no problem."

"Okay. We're headed home. Call if you hear anything. Okay?"

"Si, si. Gracias Pedro, and please tell Diego I said, thank you."

"Okay, bye." Pedro slumped in his seat, "I'm done. Let's get a few hours rest. Maybe our dumb-ass friend will magically reappear."

Chapter 11

January 1st Midnight

Finally, the digital clock over the bar changed to midnight. It was closing time and still no word from Carlos. Compulsively checking for missed messages, Yasmin was surprised to see an email with an attachment that had been sent from Carlos' phone. Her hand shot to her mouth as she clicked open a photograph.

"Oh, God no!" Yasmin exclaimed, "Jessica, look." She extended her phone towards Jessica so she could see the image of Carlos handcuffed to a pipe in a bare room. He was fiercely glaring into the camera lens.

"What the hell?" Jessica stared at the image of Carlos' angry face. "Let me see that," she said reaching out to take the smartphone, angling the screen to get a better look. "Who sent this?" she demanded.

"It came from Carlos' phone." Yasmin's voice wavered as she peered over Jessica's shoulder at the image. "Oh God, it looks like he's been hurt. I think that's dried blood on his head and neck," she said, pointing at a dark colored smear on his skin.

"Any message with the photo?" Jessica asked, as she swiped the screen, checking for messages.

"I didn't see anything. Do you?"

"Nope, nothing."

"I don't know what we should do," Yasmin said, reaching to take the phone back from Jessica. "Should we text back and ask what they want?"

"I'm just not sure that's a good idea. We don't know anything yet, just that he's being held by someone, somewhere." Considering their options, Jessica chewed on her bottom lip, then said, "You buzz the guys and wake them up. They've probably only just got to sleep." Jessica quickly surveyed the restaurant, only two customers remaining and they were in the process of leaving money on the table for their bill. The kitchen staff had started their cleanup thirty minutes before and were ready to sign out.

Jessica pointed at the roll-down security grill. "I'll put the gate down and let this last couple out the staff exit. You ring off the cash and lock it in the office safe. I'll start turning off some of the lights." Jessica turned to give Yasmin a quick hug, whispering. "He'll be fine, Yassy. We'll get him back."

With a frustrated groan, Diego rolled over in bed, disengaging his arm that had been comfortably wrapped around the soft, warm form of his slumbering wife. "God-damned phone," he muttered, swatting the screen in attempt to find the answer symbol. Too tired to care if this was a potential customer phoning in the middle of the night to book a charter, or his mom who lived two time zones to the west and could never remember that ten in the evening at her home was midnight here on Isla, he snapped testily, "What?"

Yasmin's strained voice echoed in his right ear, "Diego, Carlos is in trouble."

Sitting bolt upright in bed, he fumbled for the bedside light, making apologetic gestures at his wife, Cristina. She grimaced over her shoulder when the light woke her from a deep sleep, then turned away and sighed as she nestled deeper into the covers.

Diego lowered his voice, trying to be quieter, "What's happened, Yasmin?" he asked, swinging his legs out of bed, onto the floor.

"A photo was sent to my phone just a few minutes ago. I think Carlos has been kidnapped."

"Where are you?" Diego asked, the phone tucked under his chin while he one-handedly pulled on his shorts. Picking his dark blue shirt off the floor, he jammed one arm into a sleeve, transferred the phone to the other shoulder, and jammed the second arm into the other sleeve. Buttoning his shirt, he listened to Yasmin's answer.

"We're just closing up the *Loco Lobo*. Jessica is just letting the last two customers out the gate. We will be at my house in fifteen minutes."

"Okay. Good. I'll call Pedro and we'll meet you there." Diego said goodbye, then disconnected.

"What's wrong?" Cristina murmured sleepily, as Diego stuffed his feet into his sandals and reached for his keys on the nightstand.

"I'm sorry, my love. I have to go out. I think Carlos is in trouble." He leaned over and kissed Cristina's soft cheek, pulling the sheet up to her shoulder. "Don't worry, I'll be back soon."

"Mmmm, be careful, *mi amor*," she said as she closed her eyes, whispering, "Love you."

"Love you too," he replied, as he quietly shut the bedroom door and moved into their combined kitchen and eating area.

"*Papi?*" a small voice questioned.

"*Si*, I'm here son. What do you need?"

"A drink of water, please."

"Okay," Diego reached for a glass and put it under the spigot of the container. He filled the glass and carried it to his oldest son, José, who was sleeping in a hammock slung across their living area. The three younger children slumbered nearby in smaller hammocks, a modern adaption of the traditional Mayan cradle.

"Here you go," he whispered, "please be quiet, we don't want to wake the others." He smoothed his hand over José's forehead.

"Where are you going, *papi?*" José quietly asked, sipping at the glass of water, his curious eyes tracking his father's movements.

"Out. *Tio* Carlos needs me to help him with something."

Extending his hand with the half-full glass, José asked, "May I help you and *Tio* Carlos?" José pulled back his blanket, preparing to drop his feet out of the hammock and onto the floor.

Reaching for the glass and setting it on the tile counter, Diego smiled indulgently. "Another time, *mi hijo*. It's late, and you have to help mommy tomorrow. Remember, helping her look after your brother and sisters is part of your job."

He bent and kissed his son's head, "Go back to sleep."

"Okay," The ten-year-old said as he slipped back under the bedding, "Night-night, *papi*, I love you."

"Good night, *mi hijo*. I love you too."

Quietly navigating around his slumbering children, Diego stepped outside and turned to lock the front door. As he walked the few steps to his Jeep, he reluctantly called Pedro, waking him from a much-needed sleep. "Sorry to wake you, *hermano*. Carlos is in big trouble." Listening to Pedro's half-awake questions, he added a little impatiently, "I'll explain later. Just meet me at Yasmin's as soon as you can."

Turning the key in the ignition, he irritably grumbled. "Another middle-of-the-night adventure with Carlos. It would be nice if just once he needed our help during the daylight hours."

Chapter 12

January 2nd After midnight

Patterson punched a soiled, lumpy pillow, beating it into a useable shape. He had stolen the pillow, a thin blanket, and a ratty hammock from a work site about half a mile from where he was hiding. The workers had been occupied with pouring concrete and hadn't noticed him slip in through an entryway, stealing the poor excuse for a bed from their communal sleeping area. It was common practice for the crew to camp inside a house while it was under construction, a form of security for the materials, and cheap accommodations for the poorly paid workers.

Kirk had hung the hammock in the derelict hotel one floor down from where he had Carlos Mendoza stashed. Surviving without hot water, a proper bed, or decent food was no better than living like a common rodent, like the ugly Norway rats that liked to live near humans and their food. God, he hated those huge beady-eyed bastards. As a child, his father had frequently tormented him by tossing a rat into his cramped attic bedroom, laughing at his young son's screams of terror. "This'll make a man out of you," his father would shout as he tossed the frenzied creature inside.

He loathed his father as much as he loathed the huge rodents. The old bastard had died at the family farm near

Wenatchee when Kirk was fourteen. His scrawny neck snapped like a dry stick as he tumbled down the rickety basement stairs. The top tread had been loose for weeks and had only needed a little extra help to make the step unstable.

Kirk had warned his younger sister, Sally, to stay away from the cellar where their father stored his corn whiskey, and where the big, long-legged Brown Recluse spiders lived. Kirk said the spiders would bite her, hard, and she would certainly die a slow and painful death. He didn't want her to fall down the stairs, not that he cared about the snotty-nosed little tattletale. She had a habit of squealing on Kirk in hopes it would divert her father's beatings away from her. No, he didn't care if she was injured or even killed; he just didn't want her to spring the trap he'd set for the miserable excuse of a human being that called himself their father.

It was payback for the heartache and fear that evil bastard had caused his family, terrorizing his weak wife and two young children with frequent beatings and broken bones. Then there was the random cruelty, the hours he had spent tied up in a dark closet, messing his pants out of fear and need.

And there was the pain. The indescribable pain of both hands being firmly and repeatedly held on the blistering hot elements of the electric cooktop.

Kirk ran a finger over the crescent-shaped ridges on the palms of his hands. He had only been five years old at the time, but the memory of the searing pain and the smell of burning flesh were as fresh as if it had happened yesterday.

Now here he was, on the run from the Florida Sheriff's Department and living the high life in a hovel in Mexico. Being in the country illegally, he couldn't very well pop into a hotel and get a room, especially without a credit card or any form of identification.

If he was honest with himself, he hadn't really planned this scheme very well. It had been formed by a simmering rage that boiled over in a brief moment of opportunity. Once he had escaped the sheriff's van, he had impulsively returned to Mexico. He had intended to kidnap and kill Yasmin for revenge. Revenge against Carlos for handing him over to the sheriffs. Revenge against those two big goons that had taken him to Florida by boat, and whoever had stolen the small bag of pirate loot that had been in his pocket. Instead, the opportunity to grab Carlos presented itself, so he did.

While he'd seethed in jail, he had searched every newspaper he could get his hands on and watched every television program on the rediscovery of Pirate de Graaf's trove on Isla Mujeres. There had been no mention in any of the news reports about recovery of the bagful of treasure that he had snatched from the women.

He was certain either Carlos, or his buddies, or maybe Yasmin, knew the location of the loot. He would demand it as ransom for Mendoza, plus enough money to buy a fake passport. He would have to find a fence in Cancun to convert some of the valuables to cash, then he'd keep the rest until he was safely tucked away in another country, one without an extradition treaty with America or Mexico. Maybe one of the many pawn shops on Lopez Portillo Avenue would buy a few things. It was worth a try.

As for Mendoza, when he got what he wanted, he'd slit his throat.

"So, no police then?" Jessica asked, with a hint of uncertainty in her voice.

At the change in Jessica's tone, Sparky lifted his head, his name tag rattling on the tile floor, causing Yasmin to quickly shift her gaze from the photo of Carlos to the source of the noise. *It was only Sparky.* His brown eyes searched Jessica's face, his woolly eyebrows dancing with worry. When they had arrived at Yasmin's place, Jessica had hurried home, just a few houses away, to let Sparky out for his nightly bathroom break. Then she brought him to Yasmin's. Unlike the first few times Yasmin was around the dog, she now enjoyed his company. She wasn't a dog person, but Sparky had a way of endearing himself to everyone.

Yasmin watched as Jessica fretfully tugged her blond hair over one shoulder, plaiting it into a thick braid while she waited for Diego to respond.

"No, not yet," Diego said. He leaned with one long leg crossed over the other, his back braced against the brightly tiled work counter in Yasmin's compact kitchenette. "In bigger cities, sometimes the police officers are involved in kidnapping local businessmen for profit. We can't assume anything at this point."

"Diego's right. No police, not yet." Scowling, Pedro stood with his feet spread at a comfortable distance apart, his ropy arms overlapping his well-developed chest. "We have to wait until the kidnappers contact someone with their demands, presumably that will be you, Yasmin, since you received the photo. Then we'll decide what to do."

"Do kidnapping victims usually get released?" Yasmin's eyes locked onto Diego's as she added, putting a bit of heat into her voice, "and don't *mansplain* to me, Diego."

"Man-what?" Diego asked, his expression puzzled.

"*Mansplain*," Jessica piped up. "That's when a man explains something to a woman in a slow and patient voice, using simple words." She wasn't smiling when she offered the explanation.

"Oh," Diego answered.

"Well, do kidnap victims usually get released?" Yasmin pressed.

"It depends." Keeping his expression neutral, Diego's eyes met her intense stare full on.

"On what? What does it depend on?" Yasmin sputtered. She knew it wasn't Diego's fault that Carlos had been kidnapped, but she felt the need to vent her fear on someone, or something.

"It depends on a lot of different things, like who grabbed him. How much money they want. Is it personal, or just for profit?"

"So, we do what?" Jessica asked. "Just wait?"

"Yes, we wait," Diego turned his calm gaze on Jessica.

"Shouldn't we text back to Carlos' phone and ask what they want?" Yasmin demanded.

"No, not yet. We don't want the kidnappers to think we are panicking." Pedro said, adding, "We've been through this with another friend. Slow and easy is the best way."

"Did your other friend get released?" Yasmin asked, closely watching Pedro's face and body language.

"Yes, he did." He nodded, but Yasmin could see a remnant of pain in his deep brown eyes. Something bad had happened to that other friend.

"Pedro and I will put a quiet word out to a few close friends, people that we trust." Diego said. "It has to be kept quiet, no posting on social media, and no talking to TV or newspaper reporters. His captors will want to get their money and disappear."

Jessica fiddled with her iPhone. "Wait, what about Find My Phone? Maybe we can figure out where he is from that."

"Don't we need to know the name or something of his phone?" Yasmin asked. Her fingers flicked the screen, searching for the app, then she tried entering Carlos as the phone name. Nothing happened.

"If the bad guys are even half-way smart, they will take the battery out of his phone between messages, so that we can't track it, or them." Diego said, "But if we keep checking every few hours, maybe we'll get lucky."

Looking up from the phone, Yasmin asked, "What about his family? His mom, dad, brothers and sister? Who's going to tell them?" She hadn't formally met Carlos' family yet, but she knew who they were and had waved in passing when they came to the restaurant.

Diego dipped his head, thinking, then glanced at Pedro, "What do you think? Should I wait a few more hours, maybe around sunrise, before I break the news?"

"Si, wait a bit. This could be their last good night's sleep for a few days," Pedro said, his expression grim. "*Tio* Raúl will be on the *playa* at sunrise getting his boat ready to go fishing."

Chapter 13

January 2nd Early morning

"Let us know if you hear anything," Yasmin said, speaking softly. She didn't want her neighbors to overhear her conversation with the guys. Fortunately, it was still very early in the morning, and in all likelihood everyone in the adjacent household was still asleep. She slumped wearily against her front door frame. "And, please call me after you talk to his dad," she said, referring to Carlos without speaking his name. "This waiting is hell, pure hell."

"Will do," Diego replied quietly, leaning in to lightly buss her on the cheek. "Try to get some sleep, Yassy. It's going to be a long day."

She smiled tiredly, and lightly shook her head, "I'll have to go to the restaurant early today. I have to think of a plausible reason for him not being there, for not contacting the staff."

Diego pulled his keys out of his pocket, fiddling until he found the ignition key, then pulled open the unlocked driver's door on his Jeep. He dropped one butt cheek on the seat and dragged the rest of his body inside. For some odd reason Yasmin noticed that Diego's thickly muscled thighs barely fit under the edge of the steering wheel. A random thought flickered in her tired brain. *It looks difficult for him to get in and out of his vehicle. Why didn't he buy a vehicle with an adjustable steering wheel?*

"Right," Pedro said as he covered his yawn with a fist. "Call us immediately if you hear anything." He walked to his truck and clambered inside the vehicle. Pulling away from the curb, he briefly stuck a raised arm out the window to wave goodbye, then sped away.

Closing her front door, Yasmin engaged the deadbolt and eyed Jessica. "Should we check to see what is actually in that sack that Sparky found?" she asked softly.

In the two days since they had rediscovered the treasure, they had only given the bag a cursory look. Events with Carlos had overtaken them so quickly, and they were worried that in this thickly populated *colonia*, a neighbor walking past might glance in a window to wave a friendly greeting and inadvertently see them with the contraband. If the government authorities got wind of their discovery, the investigation merry-go-round would start up all over again. They couldn't decide what to do, so they had done nothing.

"Yes, let's see what we have, in case we need it to help Carlos," Jessica said, as she drew the curtains snugly across the street-side and kitchen windows. She flicked on more lights for better visibility.

The mere thought of finally seeing the treasure energized Yasmin. She felt as if she had drunk two cups of espresso coffee. She hurried the few steps to her bedroom and removed the soiled sack from her personal safe—the same type as the ones commonly available in hotel guestrooms, just big enough to hold a few valuables, small electronic devices, and passports. She spread a light-colored tea towel on the table and gently tipped the contents onto it, poking the dirt encrusted items with a finger.

"Oh my, look at this," Yasmin said, holding a lump of dry mud, roughly shaped in the form of a small crucifix.

Sparky seemed to recognize the smell of the dirt-encased bag that he had found. Whining with excitement, he put his front paws on a wooden chair and awkwardly boosted himself on to the seat using the power of his short but sturdy back legs. His eyes flicked back and forth between Yasmin, Jessica, and the objects on the table. Amused at his excitement, Jessica rubbed his ears, "No, little man, these aren't doggie toys."

Yasmin could feel the increased tension in the room, from Jessica's intense gaze and flushed face, to Sparky's tail-thumping interest in the sack. "It's hard to figure out if these are just lumps of dirt or mud-covered jewels. Let's rinse everything under the tap." Pointing to a cupboard on the right of the sink she said, "Can you find my vegetable strainer? We don't want to lose anything down the drain."

Jessica's lips tweaked up in a half-smile as she reached into a cupboard and pulled out the green plastic utensil, "You actually have one of these?" she said, eyeing it skeptically. "I've never known you to cook."

"I don't eat take-out every night. Sometimes I cook a proper meal," Yasmin retorted as she replaced the sink drain basket, as a secondary precaution against small items being washed away. She placed everything inside the vegetable strainer and held it under the tap. As she prodded with one finger, slowly an assortment of red, green and deep blue colors winked out from the mud.

Lifting the cross-shaped item, she murmured, "It's a jewel encrusted crucifix," she said, staring wide-eyed at the palm-sized religious relic.

"It is absolutely gorgeous." Jessica said, gently running a finger the length of the cross. "I've never seen anything like that before." She eagerly took the strainer from Yasmin's hands and tipped the remaining items onto a clean tea towel. "What else is in here?"

As Jessica bent over the wooden kitchen table for a better view of the objects, her single blond plait fell forward over one shoulder. Using two fingers, Jessica quickly sorted the pieces into separate piles. "We have nine gold coins, probably doubloons like the three we found last November and had to surrender to the authorities." Jessica pointed at the coins, "See? One side has this straight cross, and the other side has the number eight at the top. Plus, there are two silver coins of similar design," she said, as she poked the items off to the side.

"Good heavens," Yasmin said, looking at the pile of colored stones. "There are quite a few gemstones."

Jessica nodded. "Yep, it looks like we have four rubies, three emeralds, and one, two, three, four, five—yes, five—sapphires," she said, flipping her hair back over her shoulder as she straightened up.

Yasmin reverently held the crucifix in her hands, staring at the colorful items on her kitchen table. *What on earth were they going to do with these things?*

"It was raining so hard while he was digging, I never realized Sparky had uncovered so much stuff," Jessica said, smiling as her dog excitedly swished his tail at the mention of his name. She gave him an affectionate hug. "You are a smart little man. Look at all the pretty things you found."

Yasmin's eyes welled up with tears. "I pray this isn't the reason Carlos was kidnapped," she said, meeting Jessica's gaze. "I'm so worried about him, Jess."

Chapter 14

January 2nd Sunrise

"My son has been kidnapped?" Sixty-year-old Raúl Mendoza shook his head as if he was vehemently denying what Diego had just told him. "No, it's not possible. Not Carlos."

Raúl's once handsome face was rutted by the effects of age and fifty years fishing from an open boat under the searing tropical sun. He was tall for a Mayan man, a little taller than his elderly father but shorter than his three sons. An increase in protein in their meals had likely contributed to the upsurge in height with each generation. His broad shoulders and long thick muscles in his arms had been sculpted by working with the heavy fishing nets since he was a young child. He wore a tattered pair of shorts and the type of white long-sleeved t-shirt favored by the men who worked on the water. On his feet were cheap plastic thongs, costing about a dollar at the local grocery store. His work clothes were inexpensive, useful only for work and thrown out when too threadbare to wear. His deep-set brown eyes, that in normal circumstances sparkled with laughter, were scrunched with distress as he studied Diego.

Nearby but out of earshot, Raúl's crew waited for him to join them and begin the day's work. Uncomplaining, the four sun-darkened men lingered. Two stood calf deep in the water on either side of the boat, hands resting lightly on the gunwales of the *panga*, steadying it in the light surf with the bow pointing out to sea. A line mooring was casually looped over a wooden piling as an added precaution. The legs of the two outboard motors were still in the raised position, pulled clear of the sandy bottom, waiting to be lowered once the boat was pushed into deeper water.

The men watched the conversation between Raúl and Diego with expressions of mild curiosity. The other two men sat on the coral sand beach chatting quietly, content to absorb a few minutes of rest. As a crew, their first job each morning was to motor around to the far side of the island and retrieve their nets laid at sundown the night before. They fished the Great Maya Reef at night and removed the nets during the daylight hours to make room for the tourist dive boats or snorkel excursions.

Diego had arrived just as the men had put their shoulders to the hull, pushing the sturdy boat from the beach into the ocean. He had waved them down before they clambered into the boat, asking to speak to Raúl privately for a few minutes.

"I'm sorry, *Tio* Raúl," Diego replied, affectionately referring to the older man as *uncle,* as was the custom, even though Raúl wasn't really his uncle. "I've seen a photo of Carlos handcuffed in an empty building."

"*Madre de Dios*, things like that don't happen here," Raúl countered, his hand sweeping out to indicate the peaceful scene surrounding him. The bow of his *panga* bobbed in the turquoise water. The edge of the ocean was defined by a silvery sand beach and the tall palms drooping under the weight of ripe *cocos*. The rising sun tinted the morning sky with hues of purple, pink and orange. The colors were streaked and swirled like a child's finger-painting. Located on the sandy shoreline on the western side of the island, fishermen had used this protected area to moor their boats for close to two thousand years; first the Mayans, then the Spaniards, and now the Mexican fishermen, had all used this beach. At the end of the day, the island fishermen gathered to clean their catch and repair nets while they swapped stories and drank a beer or two before heading home to their families. It was an idyllic life, hidden away from the busy, crowded world.

"No one at the restaurant saw or heard from him all day yesterday." Diego scrubbed his face with both hands, willing himself to stay awake a little longer.

"Have you checked his house?" Raúl asked. Diego saw a glimmer of hope flash across his face.

"Si, we did. His car is there, but there is no sign that he came back from the New Year's Eve celebrations. Pedro is chatting with some of our friends, quietly asking if anyone has heard or seen anything unusual."

Raúl's shoulders slumped as he listened to Diego's sequence of events.

"We even checked at the hospital, thinking he might have been injured." Diego scuffed a foot in the sand, unsure of what to suggest next. "We are waiting for more information from the kidnappers, a ransom demand or instructions."

"Call Antonio. He will know what to do."

"Antonio?" Diego's eyebrows shot up in a question. "You mean Antonio Martinez, of the Mexico City Policía Federal?"

"Si," Raúl vehemently nodded his head.

"Are you sure you want to involve the policía?"

"Antonio is a trusted family friend, Diego. The four of you were inseparable all through your school years. Please, call him."

Diego studied the face of the older man before agreeing, "You're right, *Tio,* he is a good friend. I'll phone him as soon as I am someplace a little more private." He flicked a finger in the direction of the other fishermen.

Raúl looked towards the fishermen who were waiting for him to finish his personal business. "I have to tell my guys I can't work with them today."

"I don't see your truck here. Do you need a ride home?"

"Yes, I came with my men," Raúl acknowledged. "Give me a few minutes and I'll come with you."

"Si, of course, take your time. My Jeep is right there," Diego said pointing at the vehicle parked on Rueda Medina.

Raúl's eyes registered deep sadness when he looked at Diego, asking, "What will I tell his mother?"

Chapter 15

January 2nd Early morning

Patterson stiffly pulled himself out of the hammock, balancing his weight on the edge as he placed one foot and then the other onto the rough floor. Sleeping in the unfamiliar device had cramped his back and leg muscles. One hand scrubbed at the itchy stubble on his recently shaved head. Facilities for personal cleanliness were non-existent. The building was unfinished, no windows, doors, running water or toilets. Pigeons intermittently flew in through the openings, flapping frantically and crapping when they discovered their roosting area was occupied.

The only good thing about this location was the privacy. Stuck at the far southern end of the island with only one nearby neighbor, the empty land ran from the road to the ocean. At some point in the past, someone had created a garden and walkways to the shoreline; remnants could be seen mixed in with the construction debris. At night, the lights of the hotel zone in Cancun could be seen glittering along the opposite shoreline. It would have been a beautiful location had the facility been completed, but Patterson didn't have the time or the inclination to enjoy the view.

Checking the time on his phone, he headed towards the stairway and climbed to the next level where he had Mendoza secured. It was time to stir things up a bit with another message to that dark-haired bitch, Yasmin.

"Hey tough guy, wakey wakey," Kirk shouted at the form slumbering on the floor. "Smile nice for the camera." He aimed the phone lens at Carlos. "Sit up!" Patterson shouted, kicking roughly at Carlos' foot.

Carlos pulled himself into a sitting position, then extended the middle finger on both of his cuffed hands. "Up yours, *pendejo*," he growled out an angry retort, calling Patterson an asshole in Spanish.

"No hints on how to find you?" Kirk goaded him, as he clicked the photo and keyed in a short message. "I love technology."

Rubbing his flat stomach, Patterson smirked, "Well, I'm hungry. I need a nice hot breakfast, some scrambled eggs, crispy bacon and maybe hash browns. A couple of cups of hot coffee would go down good too." He glared at Carlos, "If you're hungry, hotshot, squash a few of the cockroaches, or maybe you'll get lucky and catch a pigeon. Wring its neck and you'll have pigeon sushi."

Pulling a sheaf of peso notes from his pocket, Kirk said, "Thanks for the cash by the way. It will come in handy."

Carlos remained silent, glowering at Patterson.

Leaning back against the wall, Carlos wondered, for what seemed like the hundredth time, how he was going to escape. Yasmin would be frantic after receiving the photos. Hopefully she had contacted Diego and Pedro for help. His *papi* and his two brothers, Nicolas and Roberto, would be able to handle the bad news, working with the guys to do whatever they could to secure his release. But his mom's heart could be unstable, flipping into atrial fibrillation when she was over-anxious or exhausted.

"Don't tell Mom," he whispered, to no one.

Filthy from laying on the concrete a few inches away from where he had been forced to take a leak and a dump, he stank. Lack of food was making him light-headed, but there was just no point even thinking about it. He had been trying to conserve the water in the plastic jug, so he still had at least another day's worth remaining, and then who knew what was going to happen?

The first morning of his captivity, Carlos had yanked on the pipe, leaning his weight into the shackles, before he figured out that the only thing he had accomplished was to pull the metal restraints tighter around his wrists. The nerves in his hands tingled as if he had inadvertently slept on them and reduced the blood flow to his fingers. Fearing his hands might become gangrenous if he was captive much longer, he repeatedly flexed his fingers in an attempt to lessen the pins and needles effect.

He had spent the rest of the time slumbering, the ache in his head thumping to the beat of his heart. Kirk had cracked him a good one with the baseball bat. He was sure this wasn't a normal kidnapping where there was a chance to negotiate for his freedom. Patterson appeared to be doing this for revenge, pure and simple.

Carlos studied his muscular hands, wondering if the crazy stories he had heard during guy-to-guy bullshit sessions were actually true. Was it really possible to dislocate his thumbs and slide the handcuffs off? The pain would be horrific. He grasped his left thumb with his stronger right hand, experimenting with shoving the digit sideways out of the joint. The agony made him cry out loud, bringing tears to his eyes and scaring the roosting pigeons into flight.

Hell no. He wasn't desperate enough, yet, to attempt that method of escape.

Chapter 16

January 2nd Early morning

Yasmin's phone pinged. "Jessica. Another message!" Her fingers skated across the screen, opening the photo. "Mother of God, poor Carlos," she said, staring at his defiant eyes. He looked tired and dirty. There didn't appear to be anything for him to sleep on besides the bare concrete floor. A plastic jug with a bit of water sat nearby, but she couldn't see any sign of food, not even a few pesos worth of tortillas or the ubiquitous bottle of Coca Cola consumed by Mexicans more often than water.

"What's the message say?" Jessica poked her head close to Yasmin's shoulder, trying to read the screen. She shaded the screen with one hand, reducing the glare from the overhead light.

"I have something you want. You have something I want," Yasmin turned her puzzled frown towards Jessica. "What do you suppose that means?"

"Probably someone who heard the story about us finding the treasure last November. They think we have the gold."

"Well, we do," Yasmin replied, pointing at the items visible on her table.

"Yes, but I don't think anyone knows about that," Jessica countered. "It is public knowledge that the main part of the treasure went to Mexico City. Only we know Sparky found this bag two days ago."

"Could someone have recognized us when he dragged it out from under the bush?"

"I guess it's possible." Jessica hesitated before adding, "This is a small community, and we are very identifiable after all the television and newspaper publicity." She looked at Sparky, "But when other people are around, Sparky wags his tail if he recognizes the person or *woofs* if they are strangers. He didn't do either one of those things, he just stared at his prize."

"That's true." Yasmin said, as she swiped the screen on her phone, touching Diego's contact number. "Diego. It's Yasmin."

"Have you heard from the kidnappers?"

Unseen by Diego, she nodded, agreeing, "Si, we have received another message."

"What do they want?"

"I'm not sure," she said, and read Diego the message on her phone.

"Meet me in fifteen minutes at Carlos' house. Maybe there is something there the kidnappers want."

"Should we call Pedro?" Yasmin asked.

"Not right now, he's tidying up our boat from yesterday's photography charter, and rescheduling any upcoming commitments for the next few days so we can concentrate on finding Carlos," Diego said, adding, "The three of us with Sparky can do the search."

"Okay, we'll wait for you at Carlos' place," Yasmin said as she pointed at the gems and coins, motioning for Jessica to gather them up. Jessica gently bundled everything into the clean tea towel and inserted the package into the sack. Ending the phone call, Yasmin took the bag and placed it inside her laptop safe. Feeling superstitious, she lightly patted the lock-box and whispered an entreaty for Carlos' well-being.

"Hey, boy. What's up?" Jessica questioned Sparky as he sniffed the driver's door of Carlos' oddly-parked black Porsche. A low growl rolled out from his chest. She saw Diego sweep his hand under the conch shell by the front steps as she shouted, "Do you have the key for his car?"

"No, try the driver's side, maybe it's not locked." Diego answered as he unlocked the front door and pushed it open.

Jessica tugged the driver's side door handle and the latch released. Sparky shouldered his way through the opening, growling as he scrambled into the car. "Whoa. Wait a minute," Jessica said as she tried to hold the stocky animal back. She raised her voice, "Diego, can you come here for a minute?"

When she didn't get a response, Jessica quickly glanced at Diego to see if he had heard her. He was turned towards the house, as if he was considering what was more important, search inside again, or see what she wanted. She hollered again, "Diego, something is really upsetting Sparky. Can you please come here?"

"*Claro*. Be right there." He turned around and strode rapidly to the Porsche. "What's up?" he asked.

Jessica pointed at her dog. "He's really unhappy about something in the car. Can you help me get him out so we can see what is making him so tense?"

A dark look crossed Diego's normally cheerful features. He reached inside the car and lifted the rebellious dog out. "Jess, why don't you and Yasmin take Sparky over by the house and let me check a few things?"

Jessica unhappily glanced at the front of the car where the luggage compartment was located on the Porsche 911 model. Her worried eyes found Diego's eyes. He nodded once, *yes, that.*

"Come on Sparky," she said, tugging hard on his leash, "let's give Diego some room." They didn't really have any idea of when the recently received 'proof of life' photo had actually been taken. There was nothing to indicate the date or time, just a tired looking Carlos sitting on the floor. Being Mayan, Carlos didn't normally have facial hair, so they couldn't even use the length of his whiskers as an indication of time passing.

Yasmin was rooted to the ground, her feet unable to move the short distance to the front entrance. "Come on,

Yassy. Let him look," Jessica whispered. She looped an arm around Yasmin's shoulders, pulling her and the dog back from the car, apprehensively watching as Diego reached inside to pop the trunk release and then walked to the front of the car. Sketching the sign of the cross, forehead, chest, left and right shoulders, he kissed the thumb of his closed fist and lifted the lid.

"It's okay," he said, his shoulders visibly sagging with relief as he waved them towards the car. "Bring Sparky here for a minute."

Yasmin ran to the car. She peered inside as if she had to double-check the space for herself, confirming it was unoccupied. "Oh, thank God, he's not in there."

Diego picked up Sparky and placed him inside the compartment, taking care not to bang his low-slung private-bits on the edge of the trunk. The dog was interested in the smells but not growling. "Okay, whatever is upsetting him is inside the car. Let's take another look." Diego lifted the dog out and set him on the ground.

Yasmin opened the passenger door and leaned in. "I don't see anything unusual."

Growling, Sparky jumped onto the driver's seat, his nose giving the seat a thorough going over.

"I think he recognizes the scent of whoever last drove this car," Diego said.

"Well, that's weird. The only person I have ever heard him growl at was Kirk Patterson. He hated that man." Jessica tilted her head as she watched Sparky. It really had been hate at first sight between the dog and Patterson. Jessica vigorously shook her head, "No, not possible. He died a few days ago in a vehicle accident in Florida."

Diego ran his hand through his thick, short hair. He had a baffled expression on his face. "I had planned to call a friend of ours, Antonio Martinez. His family moved to Mexico City when he was a teenager but we still keep in contact via the internet. He is now a captain in the Policía Federal. Maybe he can confirm that Patterson really is dead."

Chapter 17

January 2nd Mid-morning

"Hola, Antonio, this is Diego Avalos." Diego sat perched on the black leather sofa inside the house, elbows resting on his bent knees. He could hear the tapping of computer keys, as if the cop was multi-tasking while he answered the phone. The squawk of the police band radio droned in the background as the control center dispatched officers to investigate new problems.

"Diego! It is good to hear from you," Antonio replied. The sporadic clatter of a computer keyboard echoed over his slightly preoccupied response.

"It's been a long time, *hermano*. How are you?" Diego asked.

"I'm good. How're you?"

Diego concentrated his gaze on the floor while he sorted out in his mind what he wanted to ask Antonio. "Well, honestly I've got a bit of a situation. Is it okay to talk on this line?" Diego asked, unsure of speaking openly about the kidnapping.

"Wait, let me close my door." The receiver thumped onto the desk, and footsteps receded, then returned. "*Que pasa?*"

"Okay, first off, I have the speaker activated on my phone so that a couple of friends can listen in." Diego explained, then added, "Are you okay with that?"

"Sure, it's fine with me if you are okay with it." To Diego's ear Antonio's response sounded friendly, but short and to the point, as if he was preoccupied by something at work.

Diego took a breath and then continued, "Carlos was kidnapped shortly after midnight on New Year's Eve." Just saying the words created a spike in his pulse rate. They had been buddies since they were in diapers. He didn't want to even consider not getting his best friend back safely.

"Any ransom demand yet?" Antonio asked. His voice sounded sharper, more focused.

"Just two photos and one cryptic message." Diego tilted his face to look at Yasmin, his glance asking if he was repeating the words correctly. "I have something you want. You have something I want."

Yasmin nodded, "Yes, that's right."

"Any ideas what the kidnapper is referring to?"

"Not a clue."

"You recognize anything in the photos?"

"No, the background is either an unfinished hotel or maybe an apartment complex."

Probing for more information, Antonio asked, "Anything on Isla that would fit the description?"

"Maybe, but it could also be any one of two dozen construction sites in Cancun." Wanting to ask about Patterson, Diego changed the direction of the conversation. "Antonio, do you remember hearing about that guy Kirk Patterson, that attacked our friend Yasmin Medina when she and her co-worker, Jessica, discovered the pirate treasure a few months ago?"

"Yeah, Carlos told me a few things," Antonio answered obliquely.

"And you know about Jessica's dog, Sparky, the one that has a great nose? The dog that actually found the loot?" At the mention of his name, Sparky bounced to his feet and pushed his head under Diego's arm, demanding pats.

"Yeah?" Antonio's voice suggested he wasn't making the connection yet.

Diego buried his fingers in the thick fur at the back of Sparky's neck, scratching him affectionately while he talked to Antonio. "Well, we took the dog to Carlos' house, to help us search in case we were missing something. He went berserk over something inside the car."

"And?" Still sounding puzzled, Antonio prompted Diego to continue.

"Okay, it's a long shot, but the only person that dog ever fiercely reacted to was Kirk Patterson." Diego could hear the uncertainty in his own voice, but he was willing to pursue any bit of information that might help them find Carlos. "Can you check that online news story out of

Florida—the one that mentioned Patterson had died in a vehicle accident when the Sheriff's Department was transferring him to the state prison?" Diego listened as Antonio rattled the keyboard with his blunt fingers.

"I'm looking at the news report in the *Tampa Bay Times*," Antonio replied. "It says the coroner is fairly certain that the charred remains are the two deputies in the front of the van, and the prisoner in the back. The truck driver is still missing, leaving a bit of doubt in the coroner's mind, so tissue samples from all three bodies have been sent for DNA testing. They expect the results in two or three weeks."

"So not a definite answer then?"

"Not exactly, but probably it was Patterson in the van. But wait a moment." Antonio stopped talking while he read more of the online news. "This is odd—the shackles were broken off with the force of the collision." He banged on the computer keys for a few more seconds, then added, "Why would a prisoner who was suddenly free hang around in a burning van, unless he was knocked unconscious?"

"That does seem weird," Diego agreed. "What does your cop instinct tell you?"

"It's an extremely remote possibility, but maybe he's the one who is holding Carlos. The problem is I just don't see how a lightweight like Patterson could overpower someone as street-savvy as Carlos."

Diego glanced over at Yasmin before saying out loud what he was thinking, "Distracted by love." Diego felt badly as he watched Yasmin's face register shock, realizing that she could have been partially responsible for the kidnapping.

"The last time Yasmin saw him he was walking away from her, whistling and twirling his keys around his finger. He probably wasn't paying attention to his surroundings like he normally would."

"That could have happened," Antonio agreed. Diego could hear pages flicking as if Antonio was checking his schedule. "I have a stockpile of unused holidays, and I'll try to get there by tomorrow morning to help," the cop said. "What's your email address again? I'll send you my flight information as soon as I get a reservation."

"diegoavalos79@gmail.com, all small letters," Diego answered.

"Right, got it," Antonio said, "In the meantime try to think of locations where he might be."

Chapter 18

January 2nd Mid-morning

"I am feeling a little better knowing Captain Martinez is coming to help us," Yasmin said, huffing out a tension-filled breath. "But I still have to convince the staff at the *Loco Lobo* that things are under control."

Jessica piped up, "Tell them Carlos was unexpectedly called away on an urgent business trip."

"No, that's not going to work," Diego shook his head. "Most of the people who know him understand that business is way down on his list of priorities."

"I don't get it," said Jessica, "he's very focused making the *Loco Lobo* successful. Why wouldn't he want to deal with an urgent business problem?"

"Family, church, friends, and then work, that's the order in our hearts," Diego said, tapping his chest.

"Si, you're right Diego, family is everything," agreed Yasmin. "Everything else falls in behind."

"Okay, so should we say he was called away for a family emergency?" asked Jessica.

"Si, that's a more plausible excuse," Diego agreed. "Tell everyone Carlos' younger sister Mariana, who lives in Valladolid, has suddenly taken ill. She has been transported to Mérida with its bigger hospitals and better-trained doctors."

Jessica nodded, "Okay, that's believable."

"We'll tell them Carlos received a panicked call from his parents early on the morning of January 1st and he agreed to drive his mother to Mérida to be with his sister. His father will go later. Apparently, Carlos didn't have time to phone the *Loco Lobo*. He finally was able to send a text to Yasmin this morning, asking her to manage the restaurant while he was away."

"It's a small island, Diego. Someone will see Carlos' mom and wonder why she isn't in Mérida," Jessica said, verbally punching a hole in his story.

"Good point. I'll ask *Tio* Raúl to have either Nicolas or Roberto drive to Puerto Juarez and meet their mother as she comes off the Ultramar ferry," Diego said. "She can stay with one of her sons in Valladolid until we get this sorted out. If she leaves as soon as possible, fewer people will wonder what's up."

Diego called Carlos' dad, Raúl Mendoza, to explain their idea, obtaining his full cooperation for the plan. Diego then phoned Pedro, who was just finishing the rescheduling of their upcoming charters.

"Hey *compañero*. All done?"

Pedro answered, "Yes, headed your way. Are you still at Carlos' house?"

"Si, but I have a favor to ask. Can you follow Yasmin home and check her place?"

"Sure, does she need a ride?" asked Diego.

"No, she has her moto. Just follow her home. I'm worried that someone might be hiding inside."

"*Si, no hay problema*. Be there in a few minutes." Diego could hear Pedro walking on the wooden dock at the Bally Hoo wharf where their boat was berthed, heading towards the parking area and his Nissan pickup.

"I'll wait until you are here. Then I'll take Jessica and Sparky to her place to check for intruders."

Once Pedro confirmed her house was secure and she could enter, Yasmin gathered up a fresh change of clothes and headed into the bathroom for a quick freshen up.

Wiping the shower steam from the mirror with a corner of her towel, she stared at her reflection. She saw the face of a stressed woman who looked much older than her twenty-eight years. Her deep green eyes, her best facial feature, were dull with bags the size of small suitcases puffing up her lower eyelids. Her normally soft and curly hair looked like wet string. The natural blond streaks running through the dark brown looked brassy in the bathroom light. She looked a mess. Snorting at her vanity, Yasmin turned away from the mirror and dressed quickly.

She exited the bathroom, slipped on a pair of low-heeled sandals, and gathered her keys and cell. "I'm fine now, Pedro. I'll go straight to work from here."

"Okay, but stick to the main streets and don't take any chances," Pedro cautioned her. "If you feel threatened, yell, run, scream."

"Si, I understand." She locked her front door, waved goodbye, and then turned her red *moto* into the street, heading north.

Weaving through the traffic, Yasmin negotiated the busy street on the eastern side of the island between two popular eateries, the Caribbean Brisas Restaurante and the Mango Café. Parked cars, golf carts and trucks lined both sides of the narrow street, necessitating northbound and southbound drivers to alternate when passing the congested area. As the wheels of her *moto* bounced over the speed bump by the ice-cream parlor, she looked to her right at the serenely beautiful edifice of the Capilla de Guadalupe. Instinctively, she sketched the sign of the cross and silently prayed for Carlos to be released unharmed.

The Capilla de Guadalupe was her favorite church on the island, with its wide and welcoming entrance, sunlight streaming through the floor-to-ceiling glass wall that overlooked the turquoise ocean. The spectacular view caused more than one parishioner to lose their place in the hymnals. The front of the church was made of stones, hand-placed in the traditional hacienda style, offset by two dramatic and modernistic wings. The all-white structure looked as if it might lift away from the earth and soar to the heavens. *Surely God would hear her prayers in a place of such beauty.*

Reluctantly heading towards *Centro* and the *Loco Lobo*, Yasmin mentally prepared herself for a meeting with the other employees. She had to convince the staff that everything was okay, that Carlos would be back in a day or so. She had never been very good at hiding her feelings; her face was usually an open book for her emotions. She would have to be convincing with her story to keep the idle gossip to a manageable level, and hopefully make the kidnappers think they were willing to cooperate. If only someone would tell her what they actually wanted, she would gladly trade anything she had for Carlos.

Chapter 19

January 2nd Late-morning

Kirk Patterson slouched between two racks of shirts in a gift store on Hidalgo Avenue, next to the *Loco Lobo*. Dark sunglasses covered his unfriendly blue eyes, and a black, nondescript ball cap was pulled down low over his head. He fingered a touristy t-shirt, pretending to be considering a purchase. In the background, the store clerk nattered a stream of nonsense, suggesting a ridiculously high price for the poor-quality item. Kirk ignored the man as he watched the entrance to the *Loco Lobo*. He was doing a bit of a reconnaissance of Yasmin's schedule, figuring out the rhythm of her day since Carlos had been kidnapped.

Feeling impatient, Patterson fiddled with another cheap t-shirt, with the persistent salesman still nattering at him like an annoying little Chihuahua—yap, yap, yap. He slipped his right hand into the front pocket of his shorts, fingering the switchblade that was nestled there. He was sorely tempted to stick the knife in the idiot just to shut him up. Just as he was about to tell the guy to 'put a lid on it', he noticed Yasmin walking past the store, and turning into the restaurant. She hadn't noticed him. He sauntered across the street for a better view into the eatery, sheltering in yet another tourist gift store while he casually observed her. She appeared to be gathering the staff together for a meeting. Probably about Carlos, Kirk thought, smiling coldly.

Yasmin waved and smiled at Isabela as she walked through the restaurant. "*Hola* Bela, could I see you for five minutes?" she said pointing to Carlos' office.

"Si," Isabela answered, glancing around at the almost-empty restaurant. She slipped out from behind the bar, heading towards Carlos' small cubicle at the back of the restaurant.

Yasmin poked her head into the kitchen area where the two cooks and their helpers were prepping for the lunch crowd. "Juan, could you and your team just pop into Carlos' office for a few minutes?" she asked in a cheery voice.

An unhappy scowl greeted her request, but the man complied, wiping his hands on a cloth as he motioned at the other kitchen workers to join him. Mentally berating herself for the lapse in etiquette, Yasmin remembered too late that Juan preferred that he be addressed as Chef, and his workers be referred to as the Brigade. As a graduate of the Instituto Culinario de México in Mexico City, he sought respect from his coworkers.

The room was stuffy and crowded by the time Yasmin and the day time servers, Patti and Alexis, joined the group.

"Thank you, everyone. As you may have noticed, Carlos wasn't at work yesterday. I spoke to Carlos' father earlier this morning. There has been a medical emergency with his sister, Mariana. She has been transferred to a hospital in Mérida, and Carlos has taken his mother to be with Mariana. He won't be in to work for a few days," she said, repeating the story that she had been practicing on the way to the restaurant.

A sympathetic buzz of questions erupted.

Yasmin patted the air with her hand, motioning for a chance to answer their concerns. "Carlos has asked that we all pitch in and keep everything running smoothly at the restaurant." She smiled reassuringly at the group of employees, wishing that it was Jessica who had to make this speech. Jess was so much better at gaining people's cooperation. Even though she was unofficially considered to be the assistant manager, Yasmin felt insecure about asking her coworkers to comply with her instructions, fearing that they would be resentful of *the boss's new girlfriend* ordering them around. Regardless, she would have to repeat the same story in a few hours to the afternoon workers.

"We all have our usual jobs to do," Yasmin continued, "but if you see anything that needs attending to, please advise either Jessica or me. Keep an eye on supplies for your area. Problems with any of the major appliances like refrigerators or stoves will need to be fixed immediately," she said with a nod to the kitchen workers. "Anything that could become an urgent problem, please let us know."

Juan nodded, asking with a slight edge to his voice, "Even if you are off shift?"

"Definitely," she answered with what she hoped was a confident smile. "Jessica and I will split up our shifts.

Starting today she will come in earlier and leave after the evening rush. I'll be here from mid-afternoon until closing." Yasmin pulled out her smartphone and recited both her cell number and Jessica's number for the staff to input into their devices.

"Anyone have anything else to add?" she asked, glancing at each person to make sure they were all on-side with the situation. "Okay, let's get back to work, and keep our fingers crossed that Carlos is back in a day or two." Just as Yasmin finished speaking, she heard Jessica's cheery greeting.

"Hey guys! Where is everyone?" Jessica yelled. "Hola, hola."

"We're here Jess," Yasmin said, stepping into view. The others filed past, greeting Jessica as they headed back to their regular tasks.

"Oh, good," she stashed her bag in the employee room and then pointed at a middle-aged couple who were waiting at a table. "New arrivals, Patti. Do you want to get them, or should I?"

"On it," Patti responded.

Jessica leaned closer to Yasmin, quietly asking, "How'd the meeting go?"

"As well as can be expected. Everything is okay for the moment. No big problems yet."

"Any new messages?" Jessica asked.

"No, nothing," she answered, shaking her head as she compulsively checked the screen, hoping she hadn't missed a call from the kidnappers.

Walking with Yasmin to the entrance of the restaurant, Jessica said, "Okay, I've got this." She placed a comforting hand on Yasmin's arm, "Go home, and get some rest."

"I can't sleep. I just can't stop thinking about him."

"Just lie down, maybe you'll be able to nap."

"Blue light special. Cheaper than Walmart." The clerk at the second gift store chirped at Kirk.

Patterson turned to stare at the man, who couldn't see his angry glare hidden by the dark sunglasses. Without saying a word, Kirk stalked away and silently trailed after Yasmin as she headed north towards where she habitually parked her *moto*. She walked slowly, shoulders drooping as if she was exhausted. Kirk watched as she opened the under-seat storage compartment of her *moto* and removed her red helmet, which she secured on her head. Slipping onto the *moto* seat, Yasmin turned the key and flicked the starter before puttering away. He grinned; she probably hadn't slept since his first message with the photo of Carlos. He planned to keep the pressure on, to force her into making a mistake so that he could grab her too.

In the meantime, he needed to find an inexpensive source of food and water for himself and Mendoza. He had the two thousand pesos he had taken from Mendoza's wallet, but that wouldn't last long. He had only been goading him about the huge breakfast that he planned to eat. Glancing to his right, he noticed the OXXO convenience store, a Mexican version of the 7-11 stores. That would do.

Walking to the coolers at the back of the store, Kirk selected two large bottles of water and a couple of pre-made sandwiches labeled *pollo*, chicken. Paying at the front counter, he exited the store and settled on a nearby bench to consume his sandwich. Peeling back the plastic wrapper, he took a large bite. After chewing for a few moments, he rechecked the sandwich label. *Yep, it says chicken, but it tastes like wet dough*. Forcing himself to swallow, he washed down the soggy-bread, mystery-meat concoction with a large drink of water while thinking about what he could do to turn up the heat. *Yes, that's a good idea. Turn up the heat!*

Chapter 20

January 2nd Early afternoon

The pungent smell of a fire brought back memories of family visits to her grandparents' small ranch near Valladolid. Yasmin, her older sister Adriana, and their *papi* had relaxed in lawn chairs under the nighttime sky, drinking hot chocolate and gazing at the brilliant display overhead. Mama preferred to stay inside the comfortable house, sipping wine and chatting with daddy's parents, *Abuelo* Oscar and *Abuela* Maria.

Away from the lights of the bigger cities of Cancun and Mérida, the stars were bright and beautiful in the dark sky. *Papi* pointed out all the major constellations, telling his young daughters how the stars got their present-day names from the ancient cultures of the Greeks, Romans, and Egyptians. Then he told them stories from their Mayan heritage, how the earth was believed to be the center of the universe, fixed and unmovable, while the other celestial bodies—like the sun, moon, stars, and planets—were gods. Those gods had to be watched closely as their comings and goings controlled the future.

Smoke! Coughing harshly, Yasmin sat up, then realized her mistake and quickly slipped off the bed onto the floor. The words of an elementary school teacher reverberated in her head, "Stay low, the hot gases will rise to the ceiling." The air in her bedroom was acrid, a thick haze.

She had only laid down on her bed a few minutes before, or so it seemed, hoping to catch a bit of rest. Had she fallen asleep?

Her phone, where was it?

Her fingers scrabbled across her small bedside table. There, got it.

She punched 911 for the centralized service, recently implemented on the island.

When the line was answered, she coughed out a few words as she crawled towards her front door. "Fire. Calle Sierra. Yellow house." The smoke was thicker in the living room. Her sofa! It was on fire. The stench of the burning fabric and foam cushions was nauseating.

Smoke and haze.

This was bad, very bad.

She held her breath and scuttled past, one hand searching the space in front of her face for the exit. There. She reached up and carefully touched the metal lever-shaped handle with the back of her fingers, hot but bearable. She pulled down, swinging the door open, supplying more oxygen to the flames. She slammed it shut as she scooted outside.

Tumbling out onto the sidewalk in front of her house, Yasmin hacked hard, sounding like a four-pack-a-day smoker. Every exhalation tasted vile, a miasma of burning man-made fabrics.

"Yasmin, Yasmin!" Her neighbor shouted. "I saw smoke. What's happening?" she asked, bending to help her younger friend as she struggled to her feet.

"Fire. I called." Yasmin paused and gasped for air.

"The firefighters are volunteers; they have other jobs. It will take too long for them to get here," her neighbor said. "Ernesto!" The woman turned her head and yelled loudly, "Ernesto, come quickly."

"Maura, *que pasó?*" Ernesto asked what was happening, as he poked his head outside.

"Yasmin's house is on fire, get our hose and help."

Ernesto banged their front door fully open and raced towards the garden tap. He turned on the water and pulled the hose as far as it would reach. It was much too short.

Yasmin gasped out a few words between coughs, "Ernesto...use mine!" She waved her arm towards her outside spigot. A distant siren wailed, but it was the sound of a police siren, not the fire truck. She anxiously watched while Ernesto struggled to loosen the corroded hose coupling, then reattach it to her tap.

"Ernesto...don't breathe...that stuff," she rasped out, then pointed to the right, "Spray my sofa." Talking hurt. Her throat was sore, and her chest was tight. She couldn't catch her breath.

Her attention flicked towards the police cruiser arriving. Four cops spilled out of the car, running to help, but there was only one small hose and too many helpers.

The officer spoke into his radio, "Where are the *bomberos*, the firefighters?"

"On their way," came the reply.

"What about the ambulance?"

"On another call. They will be twenty minutes. Do you have critical injuries?"

Yasmin could see the policeman studying her, considering his answer. She flapped a feeble wave, "I'm okay. Don't worry."

"You need to go to the hospital," Maura said, handing Yasmin a wet cloth and motioning she should wipe her face.

Still scrutinizing her, the officer spoke into his radio, "No, she's stable for now."

"Just smoke," Yasmin said, her voice squeaking as she spoke. The cloth was black with soot after only one pass over her face. She needed a mirror.

"Yes, and that's dangerous. It could have damaged your lungs," her neighbor retorted.

Yasmin stubbornly shook her head, "I'm fine."

Maura threw up her hands, "We'll see about that."

The officer pointed at either end of the street, telling the constables to block off the intersection and prevent traffic from entering the crowded space.

"Do you have a propane tank?" he asked Yasmin.

"Si, a small one. There." She pointed to the left, close to the kitchen area.

The man pulled open the door to a small *bodega*, a storage area. He turned the tank valve to the off position, then disconnected and removed it.

"Alexis," he said, to the policewoman, "move this over there," he pointed across the street, "just in case."

Finally, the undulating wail of the fire siren could be heard coming closer and closer. The fire truck stopped close to her house, startling Yasmin as a sudden blast of air exploded from under the truck. *Air brakes.*

The driver opened the door and hopped to the ground, bypassing the metal step. Two other men, encumbered by bright yellow over-sized jackets, thick coveralls and knee-high water-proof boots clambered out of the passenger side. They tugged heavy tanks over their shoulders, similar to ones used by her friends when scuba-diving, and pulled on face masks. They appeared to be checking each other's equipment before pulling the large hose from the truck.

"That's it, Rodrigo?" Yasmin heard the police officer ask the driver, who she knew was a captain in the fire department, "Three guys are all that responded?"

"Si, Arturo," Rodrigo answered, "The others will be here as soon as they can." He quickly attached the hose and flipped levers, charging the hose with water.

Ernesto moved aside, allowing the men better access.

One of the men waved an arm, pointing backwards, "Move back," he shouted. At least that's what Yasmin thought he said. It was difficult to clearly understand his words through the thick glass of his face plate. She stepped back a little, but could still see what was happening inside her house.

The firefighters dragged the hose to the house, poked it inside and opened the nozzle. A heavy spray of water soaked the interior, dousing the flames.

Pulling the hose with them, the two men stomped inside, and kicked at the smouldering mess. Rodrigo held a long-handled metal tool that had a wicked looking hook at one end. He handed it to the closest firefighter. Yasmin sadly watched as the man disembowelled her favorite piece of furniture, her pretty blue sofa. Eventually they seemed satisfied with their results and carried the charred remains into the street.

Three more men dressed in their fire gear arrived in a red Nissan. They clumsily clambered out of the vehicle, advancing towards the others.

"Where do you need us, Captain?"

Pointing at the sofa, Rodrigo said, "This seems to be the source of the fire, but we still have to check the rest of the house for hot spots."

Finally, a third siren-tone could be heard, and the Red Cross ambulance arrived. The driver spoke to the police officer, while the other attendant guided Yasmin inside their van. He apologized for taking so long, saying that they had been busy with a multi-vehicle accident involving a golf cart, a moto, and a truck.

Shaking his head at the foolishness of people, the attendant told Yasmin a ten-year-old boy had been driving the golf cart. He panicked at a busy intersection and struck a motor scooter, knocking the *moto* and its passengers under the wheels of a large flatbed delivery truck.

"It was bad," the attendant said, "seven people injured, two adults and a six-month-old baby on the scooter and four people in the golf cart. We had to transport nearly everyone so both ambulances were in use. The truck driver wasn't hurt, but he was badly shaken up."

The paramedics had given Yasmin oxygen to ease her breathing, then poked and prodded, checking her blood pressure and heart rate. They advised her to go to the hospital for more tests, but she refused. She had to sort out a place to stay, and she had responsibilities at the restaurant. She could see by the look on the man's face that he thought she was foolish. It was her decision to make, not his. She signed the form declining further assistance, and the crew departed, dispatched to another accident. January was the beginning of high season for tourism on the island, and drunken silliness was rampant.

The firefighters and captain checked the structure and adjoining houses, and they pronounced it safe to return. The three late-arriving firefighters were the first to leave, returning to whatever jobs they were doing when the call came in. Rodrigo stayed behind, saying he would get a ride back to the station with Arturo. Yasmin overheard him reminding the crew to refill the water in the tanker, and sort out the equipment they had used, in preparation for the next call.

Dispirited, Yasmin wandered through her home. The lingering stench triggered a coughing fit. What a mess. Luckily for everyone in the *colonia,* the blaze had been confined to her living area. Her *casita* and those belonging to her neighbors were made of concrete, not wood. Concrete blocks were affordable and durable. Wood was expensive, difficult to obtain, and quickly devoured by tropical insects. But the aftermath of even a small fire was disheartening. Inside the house a wet, stinky haze still lingered. Black water pooled on the tile floor, dripped from walls and cupboards. Her clothes, her bedding, her towels; everything was damp and smelling of soot. It was going to take days to get this cleaned up.

Rodrigo motioned for her to come over to where he and the police officer, Arturo, were studying a window. They were looking at a multi-paned window at the front of the living room. It was the one window where she hadn't bothered to have security bars installed, thinking the openings were too small for even a bone-thin burglar to fit through.

"Was this window like this before?" the fire captain asked, pointing at the bottom corner, where one out of the nine panes of glass was missing.

She shook her head. "No," she said, wondering when she might have actually looked at the window, and not just glanced at it as she walked inside.

"Judging by the heat of the fire and the glass bits that we found on the floor, someone tossed a Molotov cocktail into your house."

"A what?" Yasmin asked, hacking. "But how?"

"It's pretty easy. It just takes something like a glass Coke bottle, a little gasoline, and a bit of cloth sticking out the top." Rodrigo demonstrated by inserting his hand through the missing pane, "Light it and toss."

"Wouldn't someone...notice?"

"Probably waited for a quiet time. If anyone saw him fiddling with the window, he could say he was fixing it for you." Rodrigo shrugged, "A few minutes to pull the glass out of the wooden frame, and then light the rag, toss the bottle, and keep on walking."

Arturo hit her with what she assumed was his well-practiced cop glare, "But more importantly, Señorita Yasmin, why would someone do this?"

"I don't know," she answered.

Chapter 21

January 2nd Early afternoon

Yasmin's eyes roamed over the now quiet street.

The police officer Arturo and fire captain Rodrigo were finally gone, after taking dozens of photos with their cellphones, and peppering her with more unanswerable questions. Several looky-loos had spilled onto the street to see what the excitement was about, and then lost interest once the firefighters left.

Ernesto and Maura had offered her a place to stay. She had politely declined, saying the late-night hours she worked would be too difficult for everyone, when in reality, it was the abundance of small children in the house that would be difficult for her right now. She loved kids, and hoped to have a few herself, but after the week from hell, a boisterous tribe of elementary-school-aged youngsters would just be too much.

She pressed the call icon on her phone and waited for the familiar voice to answer.

"Hi, Jess," she said, struggling to control her wheezing, "I've got a problem." She stopped and took a breath. "Can I stay...with you...for a few days?" In the background she could hear people talking, dishes clattering and wood scraping on the tile floors as people shifted their chairs. It sounded like the *Loco Lobo* was busy.

"Sure, what's going on?" Jessica asked.

Yasmin's throat was raw, and her words tasted of smoke. It was easier to speak if she kept her answers short. "A fire...my place," she said, attempting to keep the fear and anger out of her voice.

"What?" Yasmin heard Jessica yell the one word before a loud crash threatened the health of her eardrum.

"Damn it, I'm sorry. I dropped my phone." Jessica mumbled, then said more clearly, "Yassy, are you still there?"

"I'm here." She turned her head and coughed a few times to ease the congestion in her lungs.

"Sorry, I dropped my phone on the floor. What did you say about a fire?"

"My sofa...caught fire. There's damage...inside my house."

"Holy crap!" Jessica said, "Are you okay?"

"I'm okay. My stuff...is wet...and reeks," Yasmin rasped.

"You are talking funny. What's wrong?" Jessica sounded worried.

"Frog in my throat," Yasmin said, repeating the humorous English expression she had heard Jessica use.

"Frog? That sounds like you swallowed a huge Bull-frog," Jessica quipped. "Seriously what's wrong with your voice?"

"Smoke."

"Did you go to the hospital to get checked?" Jessica asked.

"No, not yet."

"Yasmin, smoke inhalation can cause edema of the lungs. My mom's an emergency nurse and she's always harping at my firefighter brothers when they're exposed," she said, lecturing her friend. "You need to get checked."

"Tomorrow."

"No, damn it! Now."

"Tomorrow...I promise."

"You are so damn stubborn," Jessica said with a huff. "Alright, tomorrow you get checked by a doctor, and of course you can stay with me, for as long as you want," she said.

In the background, Yasmin could hear Jessica telling Isabela about the fire.

"Isabela wants to know if she can do anything for you."

"No, I'm okay...but tell her...thank you."

"Okay, I will. Do you still have the key that I gave you?"

"Yes," Yasmin said. A few months before, after Jessica had adopted Sparky, she had given Yasmin a key to her house for, in Jessica's words, doggy-related emergencies. Jessica fussed over her stray dog as if he was a little kid. If she was delayed at work, she worried his water bowl might be empty, or he might need to pee or poop, or he might be hungry, bored, or lonely. Jessica loved her dog.

"We're roughly the same size, other than the length of our legs and size of our feet, so take whatever clothes you need."

"Thank you...so much."

There was a short lull, and Yasmin could hear Jessica walking a few steps, then she whispered, "Is everything else okay? You know, the things we stored at your house?" Jessica asked, broadly hinting at the cloth bag Sparky had found.

"I'll check...I'm sure it's okay," she said, realizing it hadn't crossed her mind. "The safe...is fireproof."

"How about your kitchen table and chairs?"

"Dirty," she said, suppressing an urge to whine.

"I'll pitch in, and I bet we can get a few others to help. Go have a long, hot shower at my place. Use lots of my mango-coconut bath gel. It'll help."

"Thank you. I'll be in...a little later."

"No. Go to bed. We can handle it."

"No, I'll be there," Yasmin said determinedly. She ended the call and stared at her wet, dirty feet tucked into her ruined leather sandals.

A small part of her wanted to give in to her exhaustion, to just collapse on the curb and have a good hard cry. To throw her cell phone as hard and far as she could and scream at the heavens, "It's not fair! It's just not fair." But she wasn't a quitter, and bawling her eyes out wouldn't fix her house, or get Carlos back, so that wasn't going to happen. Besides, her throat was too damn sore for yelling.

She reluctantly re-entered her filthy house, rooting around until she found a somewhat clean plastic bag. First thing was to locate her purse and wallet and put those inside the bag; then in the bathroom she added a few basic cosmetics, her hairbrush, and toiletries. In the bedroom she sorted through her collection of sandals until she found a pair that were clean, and added them to the sack.

She decided she couldn't risk leaving the items that Jessica was furtively referring to in a house that had a broken window. What if the guy or guys came back and decided to finish the job? Just how fireproof was that safe?

Punching in the four-digit code, Yasmin opened the mini vault; everything looked to be okay. She pulled the cloth sack out, adding it to the assortment of items that she wanted to take with her. She relocked the safe, then turned to her dresser; surely something inside the drawers would still be useable to wear today.

A small scream escaped her mouth before she could stifle it. *What the hell?* Someone was hammering at the front of her house. Firmly gripping the top of the plastic bag, she held it by her side like a weapon, ready to swing and bash someone in the head. Quietly she crept along her short hallway, peering towards the damaged window. Ernesto!

Yasmin pulled open her entrance door. "Ernesto," she said, coughing out a nervous laugh, "You...scared me."

Her neighbor jumped a little, as if he had been startled by her voice. "Yasmin, I'm so sorry. I thought you had gone."

"Soon," she said, her mouth twisted in a perplexed smile. "What're you doing?"

"I'm covering the hole with a piece of wood," he said pointing to the window. "I called my friend Pepe to come and repair your window properly, but he can't do it until tomorrow."

"Oh...thanks...so much," she said, as she covered her mouth with a hand, coughing.

Maura joined them, giving Yasmin a comforting hug, "What else can we do to help?"

"Nothing." Yasmin smiled. "I'll deal with this...tomorrow." She circled her hand to indicate the wet, burned sofa and the inside of her house.

"No, no, don't be silly, let us help." Maura looked at the sofa, "I'll call our son. He has a truck and can take that to the dump," she said, pointing at the stinking mess.

"Okay," Yasmin agreed, "thank you." She reached into the plastic bag and found her wallet. Pulling out a few hundred pesos, she extended the money to Maura. "For the window...and the dumping fees."

"Do I smell better?" Yasmin whispered to Sparky. He thumped his tail.

Two cups of hot tea laced with Yucatan honey had eased the pain in her throat, making talking a little easier. Then a long hot shower had removed the soot, although she could still smell the smoke on her breath. Her chest hurt from the repeated effort of coughing, hacking up black gunk.

"Is that a yes?" she asked, momentarily amused that she was conversing with a dog.

When she had arrived, Sparky had been happy to see her; he then spent several minutes intently sniffing her skin and clothes, investigating the unusual smells.

Her phone rang—the caller ID read 'Diego'. "Hola, Diego."

"Yasmin, Jessica just told me about the fire. How are you?"

"I'm fine," she lied, "Temporarily homeless, but okay."

Chapter 22

January 2nd Late afternoon

Carlos leaned against the rough concrete wall, listening to the sleepy drone of insects as they murmured in the afternoon heat. The warm salty air was saturated with the smell of fish and other sea life. Without his cellphone or watch, he had no idea of the time of day, but judging by the temperature, he guesstimated it was around four or five in the afternoon on his second day of captivity. He ran a hand over his face. His skin was grimy with sweat and ground in dirt from sleeping on the bare floor, but whisker-free. The advantage of being Mayan, he had little facial hair. Hairy legs absolutely. Facial hair or chest hair? Not so much. He seldom shaved his face more than once a month.

Still uncertain of his location, he could hear waves thumping against something below him, but not right below. It was a distance away from the building. It could be a big wharf, or it could be the shoreline where large pieces of the island had crumbled and fallen into the water. Or again, he could be someplace other than Isla, anywhere on the mainland within a few hours of the island and close to the ocean.

He heard a soft rubbing noise coming from the stairway, like a shoe skimming across the rough surface. "*Hola!*" he croaked. His throat was raw from yelling for help, and his meagre supply of drinking water had run out a few hours before. He coughed to clear his throat and yelled with as much force as he could muster, "Hey! Anyone there?"

"Hi honey, I'm home." Patterson's face popped around the corner, his lips pulled back in a wide, sarcastic grin that reminded Carlos of *The Joker,* the evil villain in the Batman movies. "Did you miss me?"

Carlos remained silent, staring impassively at his captor, conserving his energy.

"Nothing to say, tough guy?" Patterson pushed the bottle of water along the floor with his foot, until Carlos could just barely touch the container, pulling it towards himself with the tips of his fingers. He awkwardly unscrewed the lid, and lifted the large bottle to his lips, greedily sucking in several large mouthfuls before setting the bottle on the floor.

"I also brought you dinner," Kirk said, tossing the plastic wrapped sandwich at his captive.

Stretching his arms as far as the handcuffs would allow, he batted at the projectile headed for his face and knocked it into his lap. He caught a whiff of gasoline and raised the package to his nose. How odd. The smell seemed to linger on the Saran-like plastic wrapping but not on the food. Maybe Patterson had spilled gas on his hands while refueling a moto, or whatever vehicle he was using, if he was driving. *Whatever, it was food.*

Carlos wolfed down the sandwich in several large bites. It tasted vaguely like some type of meat, and it could have been iguana for all he cared. He chewed and swallowed the last mouthful, furtively tucking the plastic film into his side pocket. It wasn't much as far as weapons went. Maybe he could roll the plastic into a thin ligature, then pull it around Patterson's throat long enough to render him unconscious.

"Time to give your little girlfriend an update. Just to keep her interested." As Patterson activated the camera app on the iPhone, Carlos slyly rearranged the position of his thumb and fingers.

"Don't get too hopeful about someone tracking your cellphone and saving your worthless ass," Patterson said, attaching the image to a short message, then sending it. "I deactivate it in between our little photo sessions," he said, flipping the device over and removing the battery, which he shoved into his left pocket.

"You've been reading too many detective novels," Carlos said wryly. "That technology isn't available on Isla."

Patterson glowered as he appeared to be thinking about this new bit of information. Carlos hoped he believed him and wouldn't disable the phone next time he used it. It was true that the municipal police were not equipped with the latest electronic gadgets, but most personal phones now had a version of the Find My Phone app, and hopefully someone was trying to locate him.

"What is it you want?" Carlos asked, trying for a sincere and reasonable tone in his voice.

"Don't play innocent with me."

"I am serious. What exactly do you want?"

"I want the treasure you bastards stole from me."

"Treasure? You only had a switchblade in your pocket when my friends tangled with you."

"Tangled with me!" Kirk snarled. "They assaulted and kidnapped me."

"You attacked Yasmin! She still has a scar under her chin."

Patterson let out a harsh blast of breath. "Whatever, the bitch deserved it."

Pressing his lips into a straight line, Carlos shoved his anger down, willing his pulse to slow. "I repeat, you did not have anything, other than the knife, in your pockets."

"They stole the bag from my pocket!" Patterson shouted, spittle flying from his lips. "They took it!"

"Give me my phone, and I'll ask the guys."

"You think I'm that stupid?" Kirk spat back.

"No," Carlos shook his head, "no, I don't," he said, while thinking, *Yes, I was hoping you are that stupid.*

Patterson's eyes bulged, "I want the treasure!" he shouted, his voice echoing in the small space.

Calmly observing Patterson while he pitched his hissy fit, Carlos thought, *Good, maybe someone will hear the idiot shouting and call the policía.*

Sitting behind Carlos' desk at the *Loco Lobo,* Yasmin flinched when her phone pinged, announcing a new message. "Damn it," she whispered, as she fumbled to read the text.

She had spent the first part of her shift organizing invoices that needed to be paid, to occupy her mind with safe, mundane tasks. She wasn't going to think about the fire, and she wasn't going to think about how she could have died today. She hadn't told her family; it was best not to worry them. The pain was back in her throat, but she was keeping it manageable with aspirin, hot tea laced with honey, and short answers to questions.

"Is it Carlos?" Jessica asked, leaning forward to see the small screen.

"Look at his hands," Yasmin said quietly, pointing to the image. He had formed the thumb and forefinger on each hand into a circle, the diver's *okay* sign.

Jessica said, "Maybe he is signaling us that he's okay."

Yasmin said, "Mexican sign-slang. *Pendejo.*"

"Then I guess he is telling us he's okay, but the guys that have him are the *pendejos,*" Jessica quipped.

For twenty-six-year-old Jessica, humor was a conditioned reaction. Her parents and her two brothers all had high-stress public service jobs. She had learned by their example to keep a clear head when dealing with life-threatening circumstances. Fortunately for her, Yasmin understood her quirky personality, having been good friends for going on three years. She didn't appear to be insulted by Jessica's apparent insensitivity.

"The message still doesn't give us any information." Yasmin massaged her left temple with her hand, pushing at the growing headache. She was fatigued before the fire, and now she was beyond tired—she was exhausted.

"What's it say?" Jessica asked.

"Give me what I want!"

Chapter 23

January 2nd Late night

Pedro positioned himself just inside the staff entrance at the *Loco Lobo*, watchfully waiting for Yasmin to finish closing the restaurant. As worn-out as he was, he and Diego had agreed that she should be escorted to Jessica's after work, and one or the other of them would nap in the living room on Jess's dinky little couch. Diego was at home, bedded down for a few hours of sleep. They had worked out a schedule much like when they were on their boat, hours away from land—four hours sleeping, four hours on watch.

"Gracias, hermano," Yasmin said. In Mexico, good friends were considered brothers, sisters, or cousins. Pedro and Diego were her brothers in her heart. She walked towards the exit, keys in hand. "My *moto* is there." She said, pointing to the end of the block.

"No Yassy, not after what happened at your house." He shook his head, smiling tiredly, "I'll give you a ride. Diego and I will take turns watching Jessica's house until we get this situation resolved." Pointing west along Matamoros Avenue, Pedro added, "My truck is one block over."

"Thank you. But we have Sparky." She said, being frugal with words to save her throat. She locked the metal security grill, giving the lock an extra pull to ensure it was latched.

"That's good, but you will still have big smelly men camping out in the living room," he said dryly, imagining that Jessica's diminutive couch wouldn't fit his wide-bodied frame any better than Yasmin's sofa would have. *What was it with women and their choices of furniture? Pretty, but uncomfortably undersized for the average guy.*

"Two very sweet men," Yasmin said, her eyes flicking between Pedro's face and the uneven surface beneath her feet.

His teeth flashed with a grin, "Do you need anything from your casa?" He strode down the middle of the narrow one-way street while Yasmin carefully navigated the uneven and skimpy sidewalk.

"No, I'm good. Tomorrow I'll clean my house," she said, pulling a face.

"Why don't you hire someone?" asked Pedro, "I'm sure there's a young mom somewhere in your neighborhood who would like to earn a little extra money."

"Good idea," she agreed. "I'll ask my neighbors." Yasmin pulled open the door on Pedro's Nissan truck and boosted her butt on the seat. "Nice ride."

"Yeah, I like it. Although it's not exactly a chick magnet." Pedro said, pulling his thick torso in behind the steering wheel.

Leaning back against the seat, Yasmin looked over at Pedro. "I heard you and Camila split." she said, referring to his long-term girlfriend.

Pedro sighed, running a hand over his clean-shaven head, "Yeah, we're done." He had really loved Camila, but she just didn't get his lifestyle. He spun the steering wheel, glancing over his shoulder as he pulled into the one-way street, heading north towards the municipal cemetery.

"I'm sorry."

He shrugged a shoulder, pretending indifference, but his heart ached from her rejection. "It wasn't my choice."

Wanting to talk about anything but his non-existent love life, Pedro nodded towards the closed gates of the municipal graveyard. "When you and Jessica had your little drunken escapade with Mundaca's tomb, did you ever think that you would actually find his treasure?" Under the street lighting, his eyes gleamed with laughter.

Yasmin stuttered, "No...not really." Putting her hand on her throat, she said, "It hurts when I talk."

"Oh okay, you don't need to answer my questions then."

"No, it's okay. Short answers, though."

Intrigued, Pedro asked, "Okay, then what made you open his tomb?" It wasn't often that he actually had the opportunity to chat privately with Yasmin. Usually they were in a group of friends with everyone talking over each other. He preferred the quieter one-on-one conversations.

Yasmin huffed a laugh, "Tequila. Too much tequila."

"I get that, but why open the tomb?"

"It seemed like a good idea," she said, her laughter turning into a harsh cough. *"Momentito,"* she said, catching her breath. "I let my imagination get away with me. Jessica was eager to help." The long stretch of words triggered another spasm of coughing. She reached into her bag and pulled out a tepid bottle of water, and downed a few swallows in between sputtering coughs.

As Pedro turned west on Adolfo López Mateos Avenue, toward Rueda Medina, he glanced her way. "What's up?" he asked, noticing her chewing on her lower lip, her eyes downcast.

"Do you think there is a connection?" Yasmin asked. Pedro remained silent, waiting as she paused to catch her breath, "Between our treasure hunting...and the kidnapping?"

"No, I don't think so, Yassy." Pedro flicked his eyes from the side mirror, to the rearview mirror, and back to the road. "When my buddy was kidnapped, the bad guys saw him driving a sharp car and owning a busy restaurant. They decided he was an easy pay day. It's the same situation with Carlos—nice car, popular restaurant." He glanced over his left shoulder, then spun the wheel to navigate around the statue of a fisherman and his family on the corner where the Privilege Aluxes hotel and Jax Bar & Grill sat across the street from each other. "As for the fire at your house, I'm not sure how, but I think it is probably related to the kidnapping."

"But why set fire to my house," she paused to bark several harsh coughs, and sip more water, "if the people already have Carlos?"

"Are you going to get that cough looked at by a doctor?" Pedro asked, a frown stitching his dark eyebrows together. "You sound awful."

She nodded, but didn't answer.

"As for your question, I don't believe in coincidences. Too much bad stuff is happening all at once," Pedro answered, flicking a look at Yasmin and back to the road. The street ahead was temporarily blocked by the municipal garbage truck. He slowed, then stopped a short distance back. Two city employees slung heavy bags, leaking fluids and bits of food, into the box of the white stake-sided vehicle.

Pedro added, "Antonio will be here mid-day tomorrow. He has a lot more experience dealing with situations like this."

"I hope so," she said, then she went quiet. Pedro glanced at Yasmin; she was chewing her bottom lip. "I got another message tonight," she said.

He turned his head, studying her face, "Really? Why didn't you tell me sooner?"

"It's more of the same. A photo and a cryptic message."

Pedro flicked a glance at the truck in front of him, looking to see if he could move ahead. The men were still packing the shapeless bags tightly into the limited space. The heap of bags would be higher than the passenger cab before the crew would stop adding to the pile.

"What?" Pedro asked, when he heard her puff a brief chuckle.

"Carlos was holding his fingers like this," Yasmin said, forming her fore-finger and thumb into a circle with the other fingers extended out.

"The diver's okay sign?" He eased his foot onto the gas pedal and moved forward, waving at the garbage truck driver who had pulled over, allowing him to pass.

"Yes." Yasmin's voice had a small hint of amusement as one side of her mouth tilted up in a weary smile.

Pedro nodded. The 'okay' sign also translated in street-slang to *pendejo*. "Carlos still has his sense of humor. He's doing okay."

He glanced left and right. The roadway was still crowded with traffic; *motos*, private vehicles, and dozens of taxis. Many of the drivers could have been drinking recently in the handful of late-night bars and restaurants in *Centro*. Driving while drunk was still a common occurrence in Mexico, and Pedro had done it a few times himself.

He pressed on the gas pedal, increasing their speed once they were past the congested areas of the taxi stand and the darkened terminal of the Ultramar boats. The passenger ferries to and from Cancun ceased service around midnight, depending on the time of year. A lone security guard roamed the expansive premises from closing until five in the morning.

"You said there was another message with the photo. What did it say?" Pedro asked, keeping his attention on the road ahead.

"*Give me what I want.* How can we...if they won't tell us what?"

"These guys don't seem to have a clue about what they are doing." Pedro slowed for the intersection by the navy base, before resuming his way south towards Jessica's *casita* located in the colonias, about five lots away from Yasmin's house.

"Is that good or bad?" Yasmin asked.

"I don't know, but Antonio Martinez will be here tomorrow. Hopefully, he will have better insight into the situation."

Chapter 24

January 3rd Mid-morning

Antonio Martinez' flight on the Volaris Airbus from Mexico City into the Cancun airport touched down on time, taxiing towards the terminal. He hadn't been back to Isla Mujeres since he was a teenager. A career move for his math-professor father had taken the family to Mexico City just as Antonio had graduated from the federally funded *Secundaria Técnica*. His dad wanted him to follow in his footsteps, but for Antonio teaching seemed too tame.

He, Carlos, Diego, and Pedro had been teenage punks on Isla. They had engaged in petty theft and experimented with some of the milder forms of drugs until Pedro's *Tio* put a stop to their illegal behavior. That was when he had decided that he wanted to be a federal police officer instead.

Antonio's job had brought him on business to Cancun a few years before, but he hadn't had the time to visit the island. It wasn't the best of circumstances for his homecoming, but he was intrigued to see the changes that had happened in the last twenty-something years.

When the 'Fasten Seatbelt' light turned off, he stood and reached to open the overhead bin, pulling down his soft-sided travel bag. As he reached for the bag, his left arm instinctively held the front of his casual jacket closed, ensuring the empty holster remained concealed under the garment. Wearing jeans and sturdy boots, he looked like any other average working man returning home from a construction job in another city. Antonio glanced at his seat-mate, a woman who wasn't nearly tall enough to reach her own bag. "May I help you, *Abuela*?" he asked the older woman, politely calling her grandmother.

"Si, gracias," she flashed a wide sparkly grin, displaying her silver encased front teeth. "Mine is the small blue one."

Antonio smiled at the diminutive woman. Her silver-streaked black hair hung past her waist in two fat braids. She was dressed in a black blouse and black skirt, intricately decorated with embroidered birds, flowers and symbols. A colorful sash was tied around her tiny waist. She probably lived in the high mountainous state of Chiapas, on the border between the Mexican state of Oaxaca and the country of Guatemala. It was an impoverished state, with very little land suitable for agriculture. But the city of San Cristóbal de las Casas, with its historic buildings and cathedral, was one of his favorite locations to take his wife, Luisa, for a long weekend getaway, leaving their five children in the care of their indulgent grandparents. The citizens of Chiapas who had a little money often chose to keep their wealth close by, in the form of silver teeth.

"Have a good day, *Abuela*," he said, handing her the bag and allowing her to step in front of him as the line began to move forward with passengers exiting the plane. As soon as he cleared the doorway of the plane, he identified himself to airport security, advising them that he had his personal Glock 17 GEN 4 pistol in his carryon bag, and would be arming himself as soon as he stepped outside the main exit.

With his pistol secured in his shoulder holster, Antonio turned on his cell and swiped the screen to access Diego's number. Listening to the phone ringing, he scrutinized his surroundings, looking for threats. It was an ingrained habit from years of working a dangerous job in a large and potentially dangerous city. The bad guys were always out there.

"Si, bueno," Diego answered with the common telephone greeting.

"This is Tony. I'm here, at the exit for domestic flights."

"Okay, good. I am just entering the airport area. I'll be there in five minutes."

A few minutes later a black Jeep pulled up to the curb. Bending down to confirm this was Diego, Antonio grinned as he opened the door and slid into the passenger side. "Hola, hermano. Good to see you again." He palm-slapped and knuckle-bumped Diego's right hand in greeting.

"Same to you, but not the best of circumstances."

"No shit," the cop agreed. "I'm sure things have changed a lot since the last time I was on the island. How long before we get there?"

"The roads are better, that's for sure, but the traffic is much heavier. It's at least a forty-minute drive from the airport through the city to the car ferry terminal at Punta

Sam." Diego popped the car in gear and checked over his left shoulder before pulling into the lineup of taxis and passenger delivery vans. "The car ferries operate on a two-hour schedule, *más o menos,*" Diego said, waggling his hand back and forth, meaning 'more or less'.

"Two hours Mexican-time?" Antonio asked with a smile in his voice. He swiveled his head to the right, checking the passenger side mirror, then turned to the left, glancing out the back window—looking for anyone who might be showing too much interest in his arrival. Everything appeared to be okay. Satisfied, he leaned back into the comfortable seat. Traffic in Mexico was a fluid experience, no one stuck to their lanes. Everyone just moved with the flow with few accidents and very little impatience. Horn honking was rare.

Diego chuckled, "The schedule varies a little depending on the weather and the number of vehicles. Morning sailings are jammed with delivery trucks going to the island. Mid-day it is usually the gas or propane tankers, or the empty garbage packers heading back to the island." Diego shifted gears, slipping into a faster lane.

Antonio smiled at Diego's description of the car ferry crossing. "Right, I vaguely remember. My family didn't own a car, so we were rarely on that boat, and then only as foot passengers. The fare was a lot cheaper than the other boats."

"The fares for foot passengers are still much cheaper. The boats are crammed with families on weekends, coming over for a day at the beach with coolers packed with food and drinks, and dragging an assortment of kids and their water toys." Diego answered.

Antonio laughed at the familiar visuals painted by Diego's description of family outings. "You mentioned gas and propane. We get to ride on a boat carrying either a propane truck or a gas truck, or both?"

Responding to Antonio's humor and easy confidence, Diego's mouth flicked in a smile. "Si, gas and propane are actually classed as dangerous cargo. The drivers pay a huge fare to use the ferry," Diego said, turning his head to check over his left shoulder before switching lanes again. "But the company isn't legally obliged to run a separate sailing just for dangerous cargo, so the trucks are always loaded with the regular vehicles and passengers."

"Typical," Antonio replied, snorting a laugh.

"Just be happy this isn't Saturday morning."

"What happens on Saturdays?" Antonio searched his memory but he couldn't remember any Saturday morning oddities.

"The pig truck."

"The pig truck?"

"Yep, a whole truckload of unhappy pigs crosses on Saturdays. It's an interesting experience to have a panicky hog piss all over your vehicle when the window is down."

"Seriously? That happened to you?"

"Si," Diego held up two fingers. "Twice."

Antonio burst into loud laughter, "Twice! You didn't learn the first time?"

"Apparently I am a slow learner."

"Pigs and propane. Gas and garbage. I can hardly wait," Antonio said. He studied the traffic for a few minutes before finally turning the conversation to the real reason he was there.

"What's your opinion of the situation with Carlos?" he asked.

"Kidnapping for sure, but no clear idea who or why," Diego answered, as he rapidly moved from the right lane into the left and back to his original lane, bypassing a slower vehicle. "You know the guy isn't rich, just comfortable."

"His father, Don Raúl, certainly isn't well-off either, with just the one fishing boat," Antonio added. "I don't remember much about his mom's family. Any serious money there?"

"Not that I know of," Diego replied. "And you know his younger brothers, Nicolas and Roberto, don't have much. One has a vegetable farm out near Valladolid, the other one owns a *tienda*, a corner grocery store. His sister, Mariana, is married to a car repairman, so again not rich."

"Si, I know." Antonio thought for a moment, then said, "We aren't seeing the whole picture yet. Kidnapping is always about money, power, or sex." He checked the side mirror. *Nothing to worry about.* "Alright, we think we have ruled out money. How about power? Anything in that?"

"Can't think of anything. He owns one restaurant on a small island. Not exactly in the same category as someone like Carlos Slim," Diego said, referring to the wealthiest person in Mexico.

"Okay, probably not that either. What about his new girlfriend, Yasmin Medina?"

"Maybe. She's one hot looking *chica*, so maybe a jealous ex-boyfriend?" Diego stopped talking for a few moments while he squeezed his Jeep into a tight space in the traffic. "I haven't told you yet because you were traveling, but she had a problem yesterday. Someone started a fire inside her house," he said.

"Is she okay?"

"Shaken up, and inhaled a bit of smoke, but she's coping. She's moved in with her friend Jessica. All of her things inside the house will need a good cleaning, but there was no structural damage."

"The timing is too coincidental," Antonio said. His cop-antenna was twitching a warning.

"That's what we thought. So, probably related to the kidnapping somehow?"

"Probably," Antonio replied, with a thoughtful nod of his head. "What else do you know about Yasmin?"

"She comes from a good family, but again not rich, just comfortable. Her parents live in Mérida, as does her older sister Adriana, with her husband and two young sons."

Antonio did another visual scan of his surroundings, then asked, "Okay, then what about the other woman, Jessica...what was her last name? Sanderson?"

"Yes, Jessica Sanderson. She's Canadian. Her dad and two brothers are firefighters, and her mom's a nurse." Diego shrugged, "I can't imagine that she would be the reason that Carlos was grabbed."

"No, you're right," Antonio agreed. "I'm just running through a mental check-list, asking the same questions that I would ask about any of the people involved in a similar situation."

"Sure, I get it," Diego indicated a right turn into the ferry terminal at Punta Sam. "Good, not too many big trucks ahead of us. We should make the next boat." He pulled in at the end of the line behind a vegetable delivery truck, put the car in park, and shut off the engine.

Antonio reached into his pocket and pulled out his wallet, "I'll pay. How much?"

Diego held up his hand in a stop motion. "Thanks, but I don't need the money yet. They don't sell tickets until thirty minutes before the boat is due to leave." Twisting sideways in his seat, he propped one shoulder against the driver's door. "Any word on the DNA from the three Americans killed in that vehicle fire in Florida?" he asked.

"No, not yet. It's been less than a week since the accident. My buddy Chris said it could take up to two or maybe three weeks for the results."

"You have a contact in the lab?"

"No, Chris Wilkie is a Deputy with the Florida Sherriff's Department." Antonio did a quick visual sweep of the parking lot, then let his body relax into the seat. "We met at the National Police Academies Conference held in Mexico City. We went out for a few beers and really hit it off, and have kept in touch."

Diego looked politely interested, "What was the conference about?"

"Increasing cross-border cooperation between American and Mexican police forces. They also want to help us to upgrade and standardize our training programs."

"The better training is a really good idea." Diego said, "And I imagine having a personal contact in the States can be helpful."

"Yeah," Antonio agreed, thinking about the DNA testing, "it would be helpful to know one way or the other if that *pendejo* Kirk Patterson was dead, but regardless of the results, I plan to have Carlos back soon."

He added with a grim smile, "I'm not using up all of my holiday time saving his dumb ass." The reality was if they hadn't found Carlos by then, they probably weren't going to find him—at least not alive.

Chapter 25

January 3rd Mid-afternoon

The car ferry lightly bumped against the sturdy wharf at the terminal on Isla Mujeres, jostling Diego and Antonio awake from their brief naps in the vehicle. After the boat had loaded and started its return trip to the island, the men had chatted a few more minutes about Carlos, and then had agreed they needed to rest. Sleep when you can. It was a favorite maxim of police and military personnel worldwide. Antonio had worked late the night before, in preparation for leaving his job for a few days, and had been up early for the flight from Mexico City to Cancun. He knew Diego hadn't had a lot of sleep either for the last two nights.

Their ride from the Punta Sam terminal on the mainland to Isla Mujeres had been slow but uneventful. No empty, smelly garbage trucks returning to the island for another load of refuse. No trucks transporting panicky pigs. The ferry was jammed bow to stern with a variety of vehicles bringing beer, bottled water, food, snack food, and furniture to the island stores. A few cars were stuck into the mix, packed so closely together that passengers were told to walk on and off the vessel. When the boat was fully loaded, no one was able to open their vehicle doors to get in or out.

Some drivers pulled themselves out through the side windows, if they needed access to the baños or wanted a bit of fresh air or a cold beer on the top deck. Antonio and Diego had dozed most of the forty-minute crossing time.

Antonio watched with interest as one of the deck-hands flicked out his hand in an experienced movement, looping the heavy mooring line over the bollard at the front of the ship. His workmate made the same maneuver at the stern to secure the ferry to the dock, while the captain applied power to bring the boat in tight to the wharf.

Impressed, he remarked, "These guys know what they are doing."

"If they miss, their buddies holler and hoot, yelling sarcastic comments at them. Only rookies miss the bollard, and usually only once."

"Right, now that you mention it, I remember."

The rusty ramp creaked slowly into the horizontal position, temporarily connecting the boat to the wharf, allowing the vehicles to disembark. On the Punta Sam side of the crossing, Antonio had watched with amusement as the dock attendant had at first laboriously lowered and then later raised the cumbersome contraption using an antiquated method of pulling a chain hand-over-hand. The man worked first on one side of the boat, and then on the other side, until the heavy metal deck was in position. The terminal on Isla Mujeres had an old, slow electric winch that positioned the heavy steel ramp a little quicker, but not by much, than the manual method.

The First-Mate pointed at the Jeep, then flicked his finger a bit to the right, indicating it was Diego's turn to exit the ship.

The insignificant hand signal made Antonio smile. "No wasted effort there," he said.

"The deckhands make this crossing several times a day, six days a week, and most of the drivers have been on this boat hundreds of times. Everyone knows the routine," Diego said, pulling the steering wheel of the Jeep a half-turn to avoid the metal stairway that connected the upper levels to the vehicle deck.

He accelerated slowly, steering the car towards the ramp, thankful that his Jeep had a lot of clearance. Better than Carlos' low-slung Porsche that had to be aimed at a forty-five-degree angle to clear the ramp, and even then, the undercarriage dragged, making expensive screeching sounds. Diego checked that his vehicle was clear of the boat before accelerating towards the terminal exit.

"So, what's our plan?" Antonio asked, sweeping his gaze across the ferry terminal, taking in the long lines of delivery trucks and personal cars waiting to board the boat for the trip to Cancun.

"Truthfully, we're a bit stumped on what to do next," Diego answered. "Why don't we get the group together and do a little brainstorming with your added expertise."

"Sounds good. At the *Loco Lobo*? I haven't seen Carlos' restaurant yet and I'm starving. I haven't eaten since six this morning."

"No, not there. Too many employees who will want to know what's going on," Diego said. "How about another restaurant that I like, *Javi's Cantina* on Juarez Avenue?"

"Sure. Is the food good?"

"Great food, live music in the evening. It should be quiet now between the lunch crowd and the dinner crowd, give us a chance to talk."

"Okay. That works."

Diego pulled over at the open space at the end of the hardly ever used airport runway. He put the Jeep in neutral. Resting his foot on the brake pedal, he lifted his cell phone out of its storage spot in the drink-holder and swiped the screen to find Pedro's number.

"Hey bro," he said, as Pedro answered.

"You're back?" Pedro asked, on the other end of the call.

"Yep, just got back to the island. You available to meet us at *Javi's*?"

"Sure. You buying?"

"No, you cheap bastard," Diego needled his brother-in-law. "You have more money than I do."

"Hey, not my fault you and Cristina keep having kids," Pedro laughed.

"Yeah whatever. Can you call Yasmin and Jessica? See if they can meet us there too?"

"Sure. I'll meet you there in fifteen minutes or so."

Chapter 26

January 3rd Mid-afternoon

Antonio sat with his back to the wall, giving him a view of both the front and rear entrances. He surveyed the inside of the restaurant, which by his estimation probably had a maximum capacity of thirty customers, although Diego had mentioned the owners had future plans to expand into a secluded courtyard at the back of the building. The small space was bright and cheerful, decorated inexpensively with colorful fabrics and posters; chalkboards advertised the dinner and drink specials, and the musicians' schedule. Although the eatery had an air conditioner, it wasn't necessary at the moment. The sliding double doors were open to the street, bringing a bit of the local ambiance inside.

A waiter hustled over to the table, handing the men menus while asking, "What can I get you to drink? We make a killer good Isla Mule with vodka and our secret homemade ginger syrup. Interested?" he asked, with a hint of encouragement in his voice.

Antonio lightly shook his head, "It sounds good, but not right now, thanks. Just a Sol, please."

"*Dos, por favor*," Diego said. Then he asked. "Is Javi here?"

"Not at the moment. He and Marla usually get here closer to dinner time. He and his *papi* Toso are our entertainers tonight." The waiter demonstrated with a few chords played on an air-guitar.

"Okay, no worries, I was just going to say hello," Diego said. "I'll catch him another time."

As the server headed to the bar to retrieve their drinks, Antonio turned his attention to the traffic a few feet from their table. "What's with all the golf carts?" he asked, nodding at the tightly spaced line of four-passenger—and occasional six-passenger—vehicles passing by. Some were the original plain vanilla color, while others were painted red, yellow, blue, or green. One was tricked out to look like a 1957 Chevy, and another resembled a Jeep.

"Mainly day-trippers from the hotel zone in Cancun," Diego replied.

"When did it become legal to drive a golf cart on the streets?"

"It's not legal everywhere, just here, Holbox, Cozumel, and one other place—maybe Lake Chapala? I think we were teenagers when it started, so probably late eighties or early nineties."

Jabbing his chin in the direction of a passing vehicle with what looked to be a ten-year-old sitting in the driver's seat, Antonio asked, "Is it legal for young children to operate a golf cart?"

Diego snorted a derisive laugh. "Hell no, but for some reason visitors think it's cute to let their little kids drive. They seem to think Isla is a Mexican Disneyland."

"And no one does anything about it?"

"Not good for tourism to be tough on families," Diego's eyebrows quirked up, "or so I'm told," he said.

"Gracias," Antonio said, acknowledging the server as he placed the *cerveza* in front of him. "Are they all rentals?" he asked, calculating how many had passed in the few minutes he had been watching.

"The majority are, and many of the rental companies are owned by the various previous *presidentes* of Isla." Diego tilted a wry grin at Antonio, then up-ended his bottle for a long swallow of beer.

Antonio nodded, "There must be a lot of money to be made in rentals." He swigged his beer, and put the bottle on the table.

"Oh yeah," Diego agreed, "*Mucho dinero*."

"What about the carts that don't have a company logo on the side?" He probably sounded like he was interrogating Diego, but he liked to have answers to the questions humming in his brain. At times his thirst for facts annoyed his friends, but eventually they accepted his seemingly endless queries with resigned good humor.

"Lots of islanders buy second-hand carts for personal use, although getting a licence for them is a bit tricky."

"How so?"

"The licences for private carts are strictly limited. The taxi drivers' union doesn't want any more on the road," Diego said. "They look at the golf carts as competition for revenue."

Antonio's dark brown eyes flicked to movement at the entrance. His interest was drawn away from the traffic to the two women entering the café. "Looks like Pedro is here with the ladies."

Turning sideways so he could see, Diego agreed. "Si, the tall dark-haired one is Yasmin, and the blond with the colorful tattoos is Jessica," he said as the door opened and the group filed in. Standing to greet his friends, Diego pointed to the policeman and introduced him to Yasmin Medina and Jessica Sanderson merely as his friend Antonio. Everyone in the group knew he was Policía Federal, but Antonio had told Diego he didn't want to publicly broadcast that he was a cop.

"*Mucho gusto, Señorita* Medina," Antonio said courteously, "I am very sorry to hear that you had a fire inside your home yesterday."

"Gracias. Please call me Yasmin," she replied.

He smiled, dipping his head in acknowledgement.

"Pedro, you remember Tony?" Diego said, pointing again at the policeman.

"Of course. Tony," Pedro said, reaching out to give the tall, muscular cop a brief shoulder hug and a fist-bump. "Good to see you, man. Thanks for coming."

"My pleasure," he said, speaking to Pedro, but smiling directly at Jessica. Pulling out the chair beside him, he gestured at it, saying, "Please Señorita Sanderson, sit here."

Antonio leaned towards Yasmin, politely asking, "How are you feeling after the fire?"

"Fine, thank you. My throat is sore. But I'm fine," she said.

Jessica leveled a snarky glare at her friend. "Why don't you ask her what the doctor said about her cough? Oh, wait. She didn't go to the doctor. She spent the morning cleaning her house."

Yasmin looked away, avoiding Jessica's glower.

Antonio glanced at Diego, who grinned and lightly shook his head. Antonio understood the signal. *Don't say a word. Stay out of it.*

To diffuse the tension, Antonio leaned forward and spoke quietly to the group while the server was busy at the bar getting drinks for everyone. "If you don't mind, let's keep this meeting quick and quiet. I was very hungry and thought a restaurant would work for a meeting, but we really should go somewhere more private after we have had our meal."

"Good idea," agreed Diego.

"So, what's good to eat here?" Antonio asked.

"Fresh grouper, seared tuna, sliders, steaks. Everything," Pedro said, grinning slyly at Diego, "and he's buying."

Chapter 27

January 3rd Mid-afternoon

Re-energized by the delicious food and drinks, the group paid their bill, leaving a healthy tip for the waiter, and stepped into the street.

As Yasmin searched in her purse for her always elusive moto keys, her phone buzzed. Hesitantly, she checked the caller ID, worried it was another message from the kidnappers. "Isabela," she said, relief in her voice as she read the name on the screen. She touched the answer-call icon. "*Hola. Que pasa?*"

Diego turned to Jessica, "Can we get together at your place?"

Before Jessica could agree, Yasmin held up her free hand with the forefinger and thumb slightly apart, meaning *Momentito,* or *just give me a moment please.*

"Anything serious?" Diego asked when Yasmin disconnected.

"Isabela didn't say. She wants Jess and me to come to the restaurant, now," Yasmin answered as she straddled the scooter and buckled her helmet.

"We'll call you when we are headed back to my *casa*." Jessica lifted her leg over the seat and settled behind Yasmin, securing a helmet on her head.

"Sure, see you in a bit," Diego agreed. "Let us know if you need help with anything."

Revving the *moto*, Yasmin waited for an opportunity to slip into the stream of vehicles traveling north on Juarez. "Someday the streets are going to be gridlocked," she grumbled.

"Going to be?" Jessica responded. "It is already a nightmare in the afternoons." She stuck out her right arm to signal they would be turning in that direction. It was the accepted custom, the passenger more often than the driver making the gestures. Pointing with the right arm indicated the driver would be turning right. Pointing with left arm could indicate a variety of intentions; turning left, or waving hello to a friend, or signalling the following driver it was okay to pass in the no-passing area.

Parking between two other motos, Yasmin stepped into the narrow space while Jessica slithered off the back. Yasmin opened the under-seat compartment and stored the two helmets. She lowered the seat and twisted the key in the lock. "Okay, let's see what's happening."

Hidalgo Avenue was noisy and crowded with people. Restaurant greeters called to tourists, *hello, good afternoon, try our food* as they offered menus to passersby. Bistro managers inched tables and chairs closer to the pedestrian-only areas, vying for customers. The shopkeepers—hawking their t-shirts, souvenirs, bags of seashells, and painted dishes—added to the afternoon clamor. In the evening, when the roving musicians arrived to perform for the café patrons, the noise level rose dramatically; traditional groups of guitar-playing mariachis competed with the overpowering noise of street musicians and fire dancers. Most nights Hidalgo had a carnival atmosphere, exciting but making it nearly impossible to have a quiet conversation over dinner.

As they approached the corner by the *Loco Lobo,* an unpleasant smell floated towards the women. "Oh hell. That smells like sewage," Jessica said, recognizing the foul odor.

"Oh no." Yasmin said, fighting to keep her lunch, a tasty dish of Parmesan-crusted grouper, in her stomach.

Noticing a spreading puddle on the paving stones, Yasmin quickly stepped into the restaurant. "Isabela, I'll call Aguakan," she said, holding her closed fist to her ear with the thumb and pinkie finger extended in a call-me hand gesture. Carlos had a list of emergency telephone numbers posted on his office wall; numbers for the electrical, propane, water, and wastewater companies.

Swamped with drink orders, Isabela just nodded and continued working.

"When did this start, Isabela?" Jessica asked, sliding behind the bar and vigorously washing her hands before reaching for a drink order slip.

"Right when I called Yasmin," Isabela replied, her face scrunched with distaste. "We noticed the smell, and then the liquid started to flow out of the manhole cover."

"Perfect timing. The restaurant is busy and the street is flooding with human waste," Jessica said with a heavy sign. "Karma can be such a bitch sometimes."

Yasmin reappeared, "The techs are on the way. They think the pump for this area stopped working." She glanced around, "What can I do, Isabela?"

"Customers," Isabela motioned with her chin at a table of four who were trying to move away from the spreading liquid.

Yasmin scurried to help the people relocate to a higher level inside the eatery. In the tropics, storms were wet and brief, dumping vast quantities of rain before moving on quickly. A raised interior area was a common feature of most businesses in *Centro*—an area a foot or two higher than street level where patrons could stay dry during a storm, or where the merchant could stack their wares while the water drained away from the rain-flooded streets. In this case the higher level would protect the customers from the *agua negra*, the sewer water.

"What is that disgusting smell?" asked one wrinkle-faced woman. She pressed a cloth napkin taken from the table over her nose and mouth.

"The waste water system in this area has malfunctioned," Yasmin said. Speaking long sentences still caused her difficulty, triggering an urge to clear her throat or cough, but she couldn't speak what Jessica referred to as verbal-shorthand to customers. They might think she was being rude. "The water distribution company has dispatched service technicians to locate the problem," she said. "Please, follow me." Yasmin lifted two of the plates, leading the way to a different table.

"Yasmin," her hands busy with drink orders, Jessica pointed her elbow at the street. The two Aguakan employees had arrived on motos and were about to open up the manhole cover.

Yasmin settled the guests, then headed towards the street. She watched as the men levered up the heavy metal cover. One worker reluctantly laid belly down in the ever-expanding puddle and inserted his arm up to his shoulder into the access hole. He seemed to be searching for an obstruction.

"*Mierda!*" he shouted. Jerking back his arm, he quickly jumped to his feet, moving away from the hole. Giggling nervously and pointing, he spoke rapidly to his co-worker. Yasmin couldn't quite make out the words, but whatever had happened had given him a fright.

Watching the men argue, presumably over who was going to put their arm into the pump vault and clear the problem, Yasmin moved closer. "You have to fix it," she insisted quietly, her balled fists resting on her hips. "The entire street will be flooded soon." She held up her phone, "I have the *Presidente's* private number. He's my cousin. Shall I call him?" she bluffed. *Okay, not exactly her cousin, but married to a distant cousin, so close enough.* Everything was about connections, who you knew at City Hall.

The worker, who according to his embroidered name tag was Roberto, glared at her for a long moment, then lowered himself back to the pavers. He seemed to be gathering his nerve, willing himself to put his arm back in the smoky liquid. Finally, he plunged his hand under the water and moved the arm back and forth, searching.

"Hijo de la chingada!" Roberto yelled, jerking his arm up, but this time he clutched a large, distressed iguana by the tail. Shocked, the man dropped the lizard on the pavers.

His co-worker quickly placed a restraining hand on the creature, holding it securely across the neck and shoulders. Its tail lashed as it tried to power its way out from under the pressure.

Laughter and cheering erupted from the customers as the liquid level began to recede inside the manhole. The blockage was now cleared, allowing the pumps to work effectively.

Still holding the iguana pressed to the pavers, the older of the two men, whose name badge read Claudio, quirked a look at Yasmin. "Do you have something we can put this in? I don't want to release it here. It will panic and try to hide in the drain or run into the restaurant."

"Momentito," Yasmin hustled to the supply cabinet and removed an empty five-gallon bucket with a lid. She hurried back to Claudio, holding the bucket at arm's length, and offered it to him. He smirked at her reluctance to get closer to the smelly lizard.

Unable to contain her curiosity, Jessica said to Isabela, "I'll be right back," and joined the group looking at the iguana. "What are you going to do with it?" she asked.

Claudio and Roberto exchanged glances, and Claudio shrugged, "Do you want it?" he asked jokingly, as he dropped the squirming creature inside the bucket and secured the lid.

Jessica had just opened her mouth to respond, when a smooth and familiar voice said, "They taste just like chicken when you grill them."

Chapter 28

January 3rd Mid-afternoon

"Hey Luis," Jessica said, spinning around to greet the owner of the sexy voice.

She locked her amused half-smile on Luis Aguilar, her eyes soft and inviting. He was a bit taller than her, immaculately dressed, and good looking but not in a pretty-boy way. At thirty-four years old, he still had long lean muscles, and not a scrap of extra body fat. Luis was smart, funny, and single with no attachments. Last November, he had been able to negotiate with the authorities to overlook their unauthorized treasure hunting. He was one of the good guys.

"This one's been marinating in sewage," Jessica said, pointing at the dark puddle.

"So, what *are* you going to do with it?" Luis asked, turning up the wattage on his grin and crinkling the corners of his dark chocolate eyes.

Jessica reached to take the handle of the bucket from Claudio, "Whoa! This guy is unhappy." The bucket rocked back and forth with the frantic movements of the iguana.

"Luis, give me a hand, would you? We can release it in the bushes near Poc Na."

Luis glanced at his perfectly pressed chinos, his bright white shirt, and his polished shoes. Then he looked at Jessica for a long moment.

"Sure, why not?" he said, with a light-hearted shrug, "but as payment you have to go out for drinks with me on your next day off. Deal?"

"Deal." She caught the grins exchanged between the two Aguakan workers. She wasn't sure what had amused them more, her taking the smelly lizard off their hands, or her manipulating Luis into helping her.

Holding the bucket handle with one hand each, Luis and Jessica walked in the middle of the one-way street towards the *malécon* and the empty land just beyond the Poc Na Hostel. The iguana seemed to have accepted its fate, remaining motionless in the plastic container.

"I haven't seen Carlos at the restaurant for a couple of days," Luis observed. "What's he been up to?" He glanced back over his shoulder, "Car coming, Jessica," he said, tugging lightly on the handle to steer her over to the side.

Jessica moved to the walkway, watching as the vehicle passed. "He's gone to Mérida to be with his family," she said, the lie spoken as smoothly as the truth. They stepped back into the street. It was easier to walk in the middle of the road than to try and negotiate the constricted sidewalk while carrying the bucket.

"Mérida?" Luis asked, "Why? His brothers and sister live in Valladolid, and his parents are here on Isla." Stopping at the intersection of the two streets, he pointed straight ahead, "It's easier if we go this way past the Casa de Cultura," he said. "The propane delivery truck is blocking Guerrero."

"Sure," Jessica glanced to the left. The driver of the truck was unspooling the heavy hose, preparing to hand it up to his helper as he climbed a ladder to reach a rooftop tank. The street would be blocked for a few minutes, then the crew would move on to another delivery. It was the norm. Islanders accepted minor inconveniences with a 'what-can-you-do' shrug.

She turned her attention back to Luis and answered his question. "Carlos' sister, Mariana, needed to go to the hospital in Mérida. The family is with her." She hated to lie to him, but until Carlos was back, they would do whatever it took to keep him safe.

Luis' expression said he was thinking about what she had said and was not quite buying the story. Before he could question her further, she flicked a finger in the direction of the shoreline visible over the edge of the seawall. "Oh, good grief," Jessica stage-whispered, "look at that."

His gaze followed hers, and he snorted a quiet laugh. "A topless tan with white walls," he said referring to the middle-aged woman lying on her back. Her large limp breasts hung one on each side of her chest, creating a shadow on her ribs, blocking the sun's rays.

"Some sights I wish I could un-see," Jessica murmured. "Like that big-bellied tourist who recently came into the *Loco Lobo* wearing only a banana hammock."

"That would be enough to kill anyone's appetite," Luis agreed, with a derisive grunt.

At the edge of the malécon, Jessica and Luis descended the six concrete steps to the white sand of *Playa Media Luna*, Half Moon Beach. It was a beautiful but dangerous area to swim, with strong currents running towards the northern point of the island past the Mia Reef Hotel. A simple wooden cross was propped upright at the location of a recent drowning, a young Mexican man who disregarded the red flag warning and the signs in both English and Spanish. 'Dangerous. Do not swim here.' It saddened Jessica to see the reminder of a young life cut short. She noticed Luis' fingers sketch the sign of the cross, a show of respect for the dead boy.

As they moved towards a group of low bushes, the lizard became restless again, perhaps sensing freedom. They set the bucket on the edge of the sand. Luis removed the lid and slowly tipped the container onto its side. The iguana lashed its tail and sped away into the underbrush.

"Not his usual territory, but better than drowning in that filthy water," Jessica said, watching with amusement as Luis quickly stepped back, protecting his clean pants and shiny shoes.

"I'm sure he will be happy here," he said, his glance falling on the dirty plastic pail.

Jessica could almost see the words going through his head, *leave the smelly thing here.* Picking up the container and lid, Jessica said, "Give me a minute. I'll rinse this in the ocean."

As she sauntered across the beach to the edge of the water, she could feel Luis' gaze following her. She slipped off her sandals and waded calf-deep into the water. Standing sideways, she rolled the pail around a few times, washing off the worst of the smell, making sure she didn't stick her butt towards Luis' face. She knew she had a good ass, but bending over wasn't the most attractive position for anyone.

Moving back to the shore, she sniffed her hand, making sure it was clean before resting it on Luis' shoulder. She steadied herself as she dusted the sand clinging to her wet feet. "Thanks Luis," she said with an impish grin, as she pushed her feet into her sandals. "All set. Let's head back to the *Loco Lobo*."

Luis beamed. His smile was warm and good-humored. "About that drink you promised me...when is your next day off?" he asked.

Chapter 29

January 3rd Late afternoon

Jessica opened her front door and stepped inside; Sparky planted his wide fuzzy front paws on her knees, begging for scratches and pats. Even when excited to see her, he didn't yap or bark, and he wasn't an aggressive licker. On the rare occasion when they sat together quietly on the sofa, if she lightly scratched his front legs, he would lick her hand a couple of times in a canine gesture of affection. It was one of the things she appreciated, his calm demeanor.

"How's my boy?" she asked. "Come on, outside for pees and poops," she said, opening the back door leading to the small fenced-in yard. "Pees and poops."

"*Hola*, we're here," Diego said, poking his head inside.

"Hi guys, come in," Yasmin waved her hand, beckoning the three men inside, "make yourselves comfortable."

Diego studied the two-seater sofa, then leaned his wide torso against a wall in the kitchen alcove. Pedro chose a straight-backed painted chair, leaving Antonio the small sofa.

Sparky bounded back into the house, then stopped abruptly when he noticed the newcomer. Antonio held the back of his hand down low for the dog to sniff.

"Is this Sparky?" Antonio asked.

"Yes, he's my gold-sniffing buddy," Jessica replied with an indulgent grin on her face as she watched her dog investigate Antonio's hand.

"So, he's the one who found the pirate's cache last November." Antonio waited until Sparky wagged his tail indicating everything was fine, then lightly massaged the top of the dog's head. "You're a very smart and famous *perro*, aren't you?"

"Yep, that's my boy." The dog stretched out flat on the tile floor with his paws out and his head resting on them. His eyes tracked Jessica's face.

Smiling, Jessica said to the dog, "Does the tile feel cool on your boy-parts, bud?"

"Are you talking to me?" Antonio asked, a small grin spreading across his face and crinkling the corners of his eyes.

"No, not you, Antonio," she replied with a chuckle in her voice, "I was talking to my dog. He gets overheated and likes to lay belly-down on the cool floor."

"I was just making sure it wasn't me you were talking to," Antonio replied. The laughter fading from his voice, he continued, "Yasmin, tell me about the fire yesterday."

"Okay," she said, then recounted the story in short choppy sentences, punctuated by frequent sips of water from the glass on the table. She told them of waking up to a smoke-filled house, phoning the emergency number, crawling outside, her neighbors helping, the police and fire departments arriving, and then finding a broken window in her living room. She finished by asking Antonio, "Do you think the fire could be related to...the other thing?"

"Possibly," Antonio answered neutrally. "I don't believe in coincidences and two major problems occurring at the same time to people who are connected, typically indicates a link between the incidents." Antonio continued, "Jessica, Diego also mentioned that Sparky growled when you searched the inside of Carlos' car."

"Yes, he was really loud and the hair on his spine stood up in a ridge. He didn't like something inside the car."

"Have you ever seen him do that before?" Antonio asked.

"Only twice. The first time was in the Hacienda Mundaca Park when we were hiking and we ran into Kirk, who said he was taking photographs of the gardens. And it happened again in the same park when Patterson attacked Yasmin and me..." *And stole our bag of loot* died in her mouth, unsaid. Antonio was a cop. A cop that she had just met.

Yasmin added, "Sparky also went crazy...when someone broke into my *casita* the week before."

Jessica noticed Diego exchange an odd look with Pedro. Then he said, "Actually Yasmin, the dog was probably smelling Patterson that night too. Carlos told me he had found a shark-tooth pendant with a broken clasp on the floor

166

inside your front door. It looked exactly like the one that he had seen Kirk Patterson wearing." Diego stopped speaking, glancing at Antonio.

"Carlos told me," Antonio quietly confirmed.

Perplexed, Jessica glanced between Diego, Pedro, and Antonio. There was something more going on here. "Told you what?"

"Another time, okay, Jess?" Pedro asked, the message in his eyes saying *I'll tell you later, but not now.*

Jessica shot Pedro an irritated look as she opened her mouth to snap back with, *don't patronize me.* Pedro flicked his eyes sideways towards Antonio and lightly shook his head, mouthing *later.*

Jessica glanced towards Antonio. He seemed to be ignoring the by-play between Pedro and her, as he busied himself scratching the dog's back.

"Can you show me those photos again, Yasmin?" Antonio asked, "Maybe there is something in the background that will help."

Yasmin swiped the images on her phone, bringing up the first photo and handing the device to Antonio. "We think it's a construction site. Could be Isla. Could be Cancun."

"Okay, I see that. And there are just two abandoned condo or hotel projects on the island?" he asked, studying the photo, tilting his hand to view the screen from a different angle.

"Yes, just two." Yasmin answered, glancing at Diego to see if he agreed with her.

"But we haven't searched either one," Diego interjected, "We were afraid we might panic the kidnappers."

"And the other photos?"

"Just swipe the arrow, for the next image."

"Yes, I see. It's the same room and almost the same image except Carlos looks more tired and scruffier in the following photos." Antonio studied the photos swiping back to the first one, and forward again to the second and third.

"Jessica, would Sparky come with me? Would he leave you?"

"I don't know, Antonio. I suppose so." She answered, tilting her gaze to meet his. "Why do you need him?"

"I'd like to take him on a walk near these buildings."

"It would be easier for Sparky if I came with you," Jessica said. "Besides, walking with a woman and a dog might be more plausible if the kidnappers spot you." Her lips tweaked in a smile. Antonio was a gorgeous hunk of man-flesh with café-colored skin and chiselled features. Tall and well-built, he had Spaniel-soft brown eyes set in a wide face, with a good-humored smile on his lips.

"I'd rather do a little reconnaissance on my own. No one on the island knows me; I am just a guy out walking his dog."

Hiding her disappointment, Jessica reached down to scratch Sparky's ears. She glanced up to see Pedro frowning at her. "What?" she mouthed at him.

Pedro leaned closer and quietly whispered in her ear, "He's a married man with five kids."

"I. Know. That." she whispered tensely. "I'm just being pleasant."

The set expression of Pedro's face said he thought she was being more than just pleasant.

Glaring at Pedro, she said in a low and tight voice. "So, it's okay for a married man to flirt with me, but not okay for me to flirt with a married man?" She drew a deep breath, "Is that what you are saying?"

Annoyance flashed in his eyes. He shrugged his shoulders and moved a few feet away.

Miffed at Pedro's attitude, Jessica stomped away, "I'll be back in a minute," she said, banging the front door behind her. She loved Pedro like a brother, but at times he could really piss her off. He was as annoying as her two older brothers, always trying to protect her or tell her how to live her life. Men! Can't live without them, but sure as hell sometimes she didn't want to live with them.

Pushing her frustration aside, she knocked at the entrance of her neighbor Enrique's modest little *casa*. The rough concrete exterior showed bits of rebar poking up from the roof of the first floor. In time, he and Rosa planned to add another bedroom for their growing family. Mortgages for the average wage earner were difficult to obtain, and the high interest rates demanded by the lenders were beyond her comprehension. Most of her island friends preferred to build as and when they could afford to pay.

"Hola, Enrique."

Enrique opened the door and grinned at her, "Jessica! *¿Cómo está?*

"*Bien, bien. Todo bien.*" She bussed his cheek with a kiss. "*¿Y tu?*"

"I'm good." He waved her inside the comfortable dwelling. "What can I do for you?"

"I have a friend visiting from Guanajuato who would like to explore the island for an hour or so. Would it be possible for him to borrow your car?" Enrique's white two-door Nissan was common and unremarkable, much like a dozen or so other Nissans on the island. It was inconspicuous, the perfect car for Antonio to drive.

"Si, of course. If I need to go out, I can use my moto." He reached into a pocket and pulled out a set of keys, removing one. "Here, this is for the ignition. You won't need the one for the doors, the locks don't work."

"*Gracias*, Enrique, *muchas gracias*." She gave him another quick kiss on the cheek and pocketed the key. Turning towards her house, she twiddled her fingers, waving bye-bye like a pre-schooler.

"*De nada*," he replied, waving away her thanks.

Inside, Jessica handed the single key to Antonio, saying "I don't think the gas gauge works, so you should probably stop at the gas station before you do a lot of driving."

170

"Yes, I know," Antonio agreed with a grim laugh. "Most of our patrol cars have the same problem. Little or no maintenance."

Jessica patted her leg as she called Sparky, "Come here little man. Let's put your harness on." The dog helpfully lifted first his right front paw, then his left front paw, while she looped the harness around his feet. She pulled it over his chest, fastening the clip and attaching the leash. "Okay then, you are going for a ride with Antonio," she said, handing over the lead.

"Come on, pooch, let's go hunting for bad guys," Antonio said, giving a light tug. Sparky planted his feet. He looked up at Antonio, then turned his worried eyes to check with Jessica.

She reached over and took the leash, "It's okay, baby." She opened the front door, leading him towards the car as Antonio and Diego trailed behind.

Outside, Diego put his large, calloused hand on the roof of the car, as if holding it in place; his face was creased in disagreement. "I still think Pedro and I should go with you," he insisted, "in case you find Carlos and need help."

Antonio calmly met Diego's agitated frown. He smiled reassuringly as he patted his holster nestled under his left arm. "I'm just going to have a look around. I'll be fine. I have my good friend, Señor Glock, along for company."

Chapter 30

January 3rd An hour before sundown

Antonio parked the Nissan on the corner of Carlos Lazo Avenue, in front of a crowded café, *Rooster on the Go*. He planned to amble around the unfinished condo development on Playa Media Luna tonight before sunset, and then investigate the second building at Punta Sur early in the morning, just after sunrise. Stumbling around in the dark wouldn't accomplish much more than alerting the kidnappers that someone was nosing around.

At first Sparky had been unwilling to leave Jessica, but after a few minutes of riding in the car, he seemed to have decided that Antonio was okay. Or perhaps the pooch thought that anyone who took him for a car ride was his new best friend. Jessica did say the dog loved to ride on Yasmin's moto, but any form of transportation seemed to be an acceptable substitute.

As Antonio led Sparky past the Poc Na Hostel on the Caribbean side of the island, the dog stopped to sniff and pee a dozen times, leaving his marker for other male dogs to investigate. As far as a canine working partner went, Sparky was quite different from the lean, long-legged Alsatians, or German Shepherds, that the K-9 unit in Mexico

City utilized for search and seizure operations. He was low to the ground, with powerful shoulders, and even though the mutt had been neutered, he was exceptionally well-hung. A flicker of a smile tweaked Antonio's lips as he realized a few of his male friends would be jealous of the dog's equipment.

Nearing the beach, Antonio could see the sprawling three-level complex with what looked to be fifty or sixty concrete boxes stacked in what would have been a pleasing configuration if the building had been completed. He noticed one of the units on the ground floor had windows and doors. It appeared to be living quarters for someone. He slowed, peering at the rustic apartment, thinking that if someone was residing on-site, then the chance of Carlos being held here was very small, unless the watchman was working with the kidnappers.

In his peripheral vision, Antonio noticed a slim Latino man waving in greeting. He was dressed in casual khaki pants and a white shirt with the name of a security company stitched over the pocket.

Antonio stepped closer to the building to chat with him. "*Hola, buenos tardes,*" he said with a sociable nod.

"*Muy buenos tardes,*" the man answered, a large white-toothed smile lighting his face. "How are you today, my friend?"

Antonio smiled indulgently at the overly-familiar greeting from the stranger. "I am very well, and you?" he politely asked, as Sparky sniffed the man's shoes.

"*Bien, bien. Todo bien.*"

"Do you live here?" Antonio asked casually, lifting one finger to indicate the ground-floor unit.

He nodded his head, "Si, I am the caretaker."

"What is this?" Antonio asked as he gestured, pretending he was clueless about the structure.

"This, my friend, is the tragic end of one man's dreams," the man said with a shake of his head. Antonio noticed a sparkle in his eyes, as if he was happy to have an interested listener to entertain for a few minutes in his long and boring day. "Would you like to see inside the building?" the security guard asked.

Keeping a relaxed and friendly expression on his face, Antonio glanced briefly at the empty structure, and then back again at the man. *Was this a trap? Had the man figured out so soon that he was searching for Carlos?* "It's just an empty building, isn't it?" he asked, acting as if he wasn't all that interested.

"Yes, but the view from the roof is beautiful, the crescent-shaped beach and the setting sun as it lights the turquoise waves," the stranger said as he crossed his hands over his heart. "Divine."

"Sure, lead the way," Antonio agreed, realizing this was a plausible excuse to get Sparky inside for a good sniff around. He unclipped the dog's harness before following the man. He didn't want to be encumbered with holding a leash in case he needed to react swiftly, either reaching for his Glock, or avoiding a fist. The man looked fit, but he wasn't activating Antonio's bad-guy sensors, yet.

"My name is Marco," the security man said as he turned to enter the building.

"Nice to meet you. Mine's Tony."

"A pleasure to meet you Tony," Marco replied as he moved towards the stairway. "Of course, you will have to climb the stairs to the roof. There are no elevators."

"No problem," Antonio said, quickly scanning the corners of the room before he followed Marco. "I could use the exercise," he quipped.

Sparky scooted ahead of the men, leading the way. Antonio watched the dog for any signs of sudden interest in a smell or a noise. A happy reaction would likely indicate Carlos was in the building, whereas a tense response might indicate that Patterson or other threats were nearby. The pooch seemed calm and content to be exploring new territory. He quietly chuckled at the dog's stair climbing technique. Both of his front feet would hit the step, then his muscular back legs would bunch under him to push him higher as the front paws repositioned on the next tread. He resembled a rabbit hopping uphill.

"I'm sorry, I missed what you said," Antonio replied to the man's question.

"I was just asking where you are from."

"Valladolid," he said, repeating the first name that came to mind.

"A beautiful city, and so close to the ancient Mayan pyramid, Chichen Itza."

"Yes, it is beautiful."

"Have you lived there a long time?"

"I moved there quite recently," Antonio answered, wishing Marco would stop peppering him with personal questions. He wanted to concentrate on his surroundings. Arriving at the entrance to the second floor, he poked his head into the foyer, noting several doorways leading to the unfinished apartments. "Do you get many squatters crashing here at night?"

"Crashing?" Marco asked, sounding perplexed as he continued to climb the stairs to the third level.

"Living here, camping out," Antonio clarified.

"Oh, no, not often. That's why I live here, to ensure squatters do not take over the building." He stopped at the landing for the third floor; his eyes were sad as he said, "It is the way the poor of the world cope, isn't it? Living in abandoned buildings."

"Yes," Antonio agreed, thinking of the huge ugly shantytown in Mexico City. Once again, he did a quick check of the landing before following Marco to the rooftop. Sparky now trailed behind, his tongue hanging down. "Come on perrito, you can do it," Antonio encouraged, chuckling at the sight of the dog's package banging against each step of the staircase. It must be tough to be so short legged, he thought.

"Well, here we are at the perfect time to see the glorious sunset." Marco stepped out onto the roof, sweeping his arms in an arc to encompass both sides of the building. Sparky stepped onto the roof and commenced a nose-to-the-floor sweep of the odorous deposits left by roosting pigeons and seagulls.

Confirming the dog seemed relaxed and unworried, Antonio studied the multi-colored sky over the northern end of the island. Hues of pink, purple, orange and yellow bathed the clouds. The ocean waves were highlighted by the sun, turning the crests a luminous white as they curled over the cerulean blue water. What a spectacular vantage point. "Beautiful," he agreed, "very beautiful."

Marco pointed at the beach below, "This is the best vantage point to watch the *tortugas* during nesting season."

Interested, Antonio turned his head towards Marco, asking, "Sea turtles?"

"Yes, the giant turtles."

Antonio had heard the stories of the local fisherman who, since the island was first settled in the 1540s, captured the sea-going reptiles to sustain their families with the meat and the eggs. The turtles were on the endangered list and rarely seen by the time he had moved away from the island.

"Are the turtles here now?" Antonio asked. It would be fascinating to see a mama turtle laying her eggs. He knew the hunting of turtles had been banned in America and in Mexico many years before. The stiff jail sentences slowed the harvesting of the *tortugas* somewhat, but didn't stop it entirely. There were restaurants in both countries surreptitiously serving the meat. Poachers occasionally managed to raid the nests, stealing the eggs, falsely believed to be an aphrodisiac for men. *Stupid buggers. If they couldn't get it up, why didn't they just take the little blue pill,*

Viagra? It's available at every pharmacy in Mexico without a prescription.

"No, this is only January," Marco said, shaking his head. "They return in early May to mate in the currents of Punta Sur."

"After the turtles mate, then what happens?" Antonio asked, studying Marco's face. He didn't seem to be acting suspiciously, he merely continued with his story about the turtles.

"The females come ashore at night to dig deep holes in the sand. They each lay about a hundred eggs and then return to the sea."

"How long for the eggs to hatch?" Antonio asked. His eyes watchfully checked his surroundings. His wife Luisa complained that he never relaxed, even when making love to her. He agreed, but lowering his vigilance could get him killed.

"Sixty days," Marco wagged his hand back and forth in a gesture meaning more or less. "All the babies in a nest hatch on the same day, and dig through the sand to the surface. Then the babies flipper their way across the sand to the sea."

"How big are they?"

"Small enough to fit in the palm of my hand," Marco replied, holding one hand palm up while he pointed at it.

"Then what happens?" Antonio asked, shifting his head as he swiveled around to check on Sparky. *All good there*. The dog was still fascinated by the bird droppings on the roof.

"Many of the babies are scooped up by the gulls and frigate birds on their way to the ocean. Others are eaten by bigger fish."

"It doesn't sound like they have much of a chance."

Marco shrugged a single shoulder, "That is the responsibility of *Itzam K'an Ahk*; he controls their destiny."

"*Itzam K'an Ahk*?" Antonio raised one eyebrow, questioning.

"The Mayan god of turtles," Marco flashed a wide grin, displaying his straight white teeth, "who gets a little help from the people at the *Tortugranja*."

The comment caused Antonio's lips to quirk up in a bemused smile, "The Turtle Farm?"

Marco shrugged his shoulders philosophically, "Even a god sometimes needs assistance. The employees collect the eggs from the nests, hatch the eggs, and return the babies to the same beach. When the turtles are old enough to mate perhaps one in a thousand will return to the island and start the cycle all over again."

Antonio smiled. It was a fascinating story, but he had about ten minutes remaining of daylight, and he had no intention of walking through a dark, unfamiliar building with a stranger at his back. "Thank you, Marco, this has been very interesting, but I must get going." He motioned at the stairway, "Please, after you."

Marco nodded his thanks and stepped through the entry, descending the stairs more rapidly than they had ascended. Antonio noted that Sparky was also quicker on the way down. Everything was tucked closer to his stomach and not catching on each step.

Shaking hands outside the building, Antonio thanked Marco again for his time, then reattached the leash to Sparky's harness. Walking swiftly towards the borrowed car, he thumbed a group text to Diego and the others. *Nothing here. Meet at Jessica's in fifteen minutes?*

Chapter 31

January 3rd Late night

Fatigued, Jessica ran her hands through her hair. She always kept her thick tresses under control when working at the restaurant because no one wanted to find a long hair in their food, but here at home she could relax. She pulled the braid apart and shook it loose, wishing she had someone to give her a vigorous scalp and shoulder massage.

Her lips tweaked up at the corners, amused at the sight of the three sizable men, plus Yasmin, Sparky and herself, once again jammed into her *casita*. Her neighborhood in the *colonias* was where tiny store-front businesses intermingled with equally cramped living spaces; where the dentist's office was tucked behind the air conditioning and appliance repair shop, and the upholsterer was located beside the aluminum window fabricator. She and Yasmin loved living in the crowded and boisterous neighborhood. They knew their neighbors and the neighbors knew them. It was home.

"Anyone want a beer? Glass of wine? Water?" Jessica asked, holding the door open on the refrigerator while she scanned its meager contents.

"Sure, a beer sounds good," Antonio said, once again claiming the narrow two-seater sofa. He stuck his legs straight out and crossed them at the ankles.

"Anyone hungry?" Pedro asked.

"Lunch was a long time ago. How about we order in?" Diego suggested, his stomach rumbling at the suggestion of food.

"Sure, I'm in. Whatever everyone wants is fine with me," agreed Pedro. "Being single, I'm happy to eat whenever I can."

"Not pizza," Yasmin said.

"Do you ever actually cook anything, Jess?" Pedro asked, fanning the stack of take-out menus on Jessica's counter-top.

"I know how to boil water," she shot back. She had quickly gotten over her irritation with Pedro, and they were back to their friendly habit of bantering like siblings. He even ate as much as her tall, muscular brothers, Jake and Matt.

"Right," Pedro laughed, picking up the menu from a nearby taqueria. "How about an assortment of chicken, beef, and pork tacos plus a few *empanadas*?"

Getting nods of agreement from the others, Jessica punched in the number printed on the menu; when the restaurant picked up, she rattled off a list of food items and a description of her home—orange and pink with a turquoise door, located in *colonia* La Gloria, across from the school.

Addresses were difficult to locate on Isla. The proper legal description and address was on the annual homeowners' property tax invoice, but owners weren't required to post the address on their buildings. Many foreigners were bewildered by the lack of formality, preferring to name their residences for identification purposes. To make it even more confusing, the signs for street names were few and far between. Many had rusted away or fallen to the ground. Savvy locals relied on descriptions, including nearby landmarks and house colors. Having a distinctive paint combination like hers made deliveries easier.

"Thirty minutes," Jessica said, ending the call and placing her cell on the counter. Turning to Antonio, she asked, "What's the plan now? Should we get the local police involved? Or the state police?"

Antonio shook his head, "No, not yet, Jessica," he said firmly. "You are thinking like a *gringa*," he added. "Not all of the police can be trusted, and I don't have any personal contacts in this municipality."

Jessica opened her mouth to argue with him, but was interrupted by the ping of an incoming text. She snatched her phone from the counter, checking the screen. Nothing. Glancing hopefully at the others, she watched as Yasmin's face paled. "What does it say, Yassy?"

Biting her bottom lip, Yasmin turned the device towards Jessica. Typed in capital letters, the sender's anger was clear. 'I WANT THE TREASURE NOW!!!'

"Oh damn," Jessica muttered, her heart racing, her face guilty.

She could feel Antonio's gaze searching her face. "What aren't you telling us?" he quietly demanded.

"Jess. What's up?" Diego asked, his expression puzzled.

Jessica tugged a strand of her hair over her shoulder, her fingertips fiddling with the ends. It was a nervous habit left over from elementary school, a reaction to being scolded for inattention, for day-dreaming. She quickly glanced at Yasmin, obtaining her agreement before replying, "A few days ago Sparky helped us find the things that Kirk snatched from us. The sack must have fallen out of his pocket when he was running out of the park. Sparky found it behind a bush near the entrance gates."

"And when exactly did you plan to mention this small detail?" Antonio's voice was low and cold. His pupils were dilated wide-open, making his friendly brown eyes appear black and angry. Jessica boldly held his gaze. She was embarrassed that they hadn't revealed the treasure sooner, but she wasn't going to be cowed by him.

"We planned to tell everyone as soon as we figured out Carlos had been taken. But then we heard you were coming to Isla, Antonio, and that scared us."

"Why?" Antonio asked, disbelief in his voice.

"You're a cop. We don't know you," Jessica said defiantly.

"Keeping the treasure is illegal," he said, stating the obvious.

"Yes, it is," Jessica replied with a bit of heat in her voice, "but, we located the cache and the government claimed it all. In other countries, we would have been given ten percent of the value as our finder's fee." Her hands waved angrily in the air. "Here, they threatened to deport me and toss Yasmin in jail." Sparky scrambled to his feet, supportively leaning his compact body against her leg, his fuzzy eyebrows dancing with worry. She leaned over and ran her fingers through his thick fur, murmuring, "Shhh, it's okay baby, it's okay."

Silence greeted her outburst. Then Antonio said, "We'll continue this discussion later. But for now, where are the things the kidnappers are demanding?"

"They were at my house, in my safe," Yasmin admitted, coughing lightly, "after the fire I moved them into Jessica's."

Just looking at their faces, Jessica knew they had disappointed the guys by not coming clean at the beginning. It wasn't greed that made her keep quiet, it was exactly what she had said to Antonio; she didn't know him.

Jessica said, "Look, we're sorry. Yasmin and I didn't mean to create problems. The situation just got out of hand." She continued, "We are exhausted from the stress and we're confused on how to best help Carlos. We're probably not always making the best decisions."

Diego dropped his eyes, refusing to meet Jessica's gaze. She watched his broad chest expand and contract as he took several deep breaths. It was a familiar tactic, one she had seen him use occasionally to release tension, to calm himself.

Chapter 32

January 4th After mid-night

Pedro unconsciously sucked in his breath, "*Madre de Dios*," he whispered, quickly sketching the sign of the cross as he watched Jessica reverently unwrap the jewel-encrusted crucifix.

"Absolutely stunning," Diego whispered at the sight of the ancient artifact.

Then she gently tilted the bag, tumbling the remaining items on to the clean tea towel spread on the table. The gems and coins winked in the overhead lights.

"Is this everything?" probed Antonio, a hint of distrust in his voice. He had been quiet, bordering on hostile, since discovering that they hadn't been entirely forthcoming until now.

"Yes, Antonio, this is everything," Yasmin said, realizing he had no reason to believe either Jessica or her at this point. He was a cop, trained to be distrustful.

"Alright," Antonio stared at the jewels. "Since the kidnapper is demanding the return of the treasure it has to be someone that knew about it. The kidnapper could be either Kirk Patterson or someone working with him. It could even be someone he confided to while he was in jail in Florida, before they tried to transfer him to the state prison."

"We should eat before the food gets cold." Pedro lifted the lid on a take-out box, checking the contents. "Do you think he could have staged his own death with the accident?"

When the food had arrived, only Jessica had gone to answer the door, making sure none of the artifacts were visible to the delivery person.

"Quite likely," Antonio agreed, "although I am pretty sure it was just a lucky coincidence that there was a crash and he was able to escape the prison transfer van." He reached for an empanada, taking a big bite before setting the remainder on his plate. He chewed the food a few times and washed it down with a swig of beer. "We won't know for certain that it was him until the DNA results come back from the lab, and frankly we don't have time to wait for the answer. The quicker we find Carlos or negotiate for his freedom, the better."

"What do we do now?" Yasmin asked. As the guys began to pick at the food, Yasmin could still feel the tension, a feeling of disappointment and suspicion. She wasn't sure how to regain their confidence.

"Have you tried to send a text to that cell phone?" Antonio asked, wiping his mouth and fingers on a napkin.

"No, we haven't. We talked it over and decided to try the Find My Phone app instead. We've tried it a few times, but it doesn't connect." She shook her head, frustrated with their lack of results. She listlessly put her plate on the counter. Food had no appeal to her right now.

Antonio held out his hand, "May I see that last message, please?"

Yasmin picked up her cell and unlocked the screen. She scrolled through her recent messages, handing the phone to Antonio when the one she was looking for appeared. "It's from Carlos' number, again."

"Okay, let's try this." He thumbed a quick message. "Where? When?" Antonio stared at the silent device, waiting. He set it down on the table, but it stubbornly remained silent. "It is probably turned off or the battery pulled out between messages." He said, "Everyone knows that trick from watching cop dramas on television."

"What are you going to do if you get an answer?" Diego asked.

"Agree to meet him, or at least agree that Yasmin will meet him with the treasure," Antonio replied. "But of course, it won't be Yasmin, it will be me.

"Everything?" Diego pointed at the crucifix, "Even that? It belongs in a museum or a church."

"It all belongs in a museum," Antonio firmly corrected Diego, then asked Yasmin, "Is it possible that anyone knows exactly what you found in that bag?"

She shrugged, "I have no idea. What do you think Jess?"

"When Sparky dug up the treasure it was in the middle of a rain storm and we could hardly see, plus everything was caked in mud. Patterson grabbed the sack and ran before we had a chance to look." Jessica leaned back against the kitchen counter, her arms defensively crossed over her chest, "We have no idea how long he had the bag, or if he even looked in it."

Diego shuffled his feet and peered at Yasmin.

"What?" Yasmin asked, realizing he was embarrassed.

Diego glanced at Pedro, who slightly tilted his head, nodding agreement. "Well, since you confessed your secret, I guess we had better come clean as well." He looked at Antonio, "You want to step outside for a few minutes, get a breath of air?"

The edges of Antonio's lips flicked in a wry grimace, "Go ahead. I'm already up to my ass in this mess."

"Okay, your decision." Diego continued, "Yesterday, do you remember we were talking about how Sparky reacted to the break-in at Yasmin's house in November?"

"Yes," Yasmin and Jessica answered in unison.

"Well, what we didn't tell you was, when Carlos found that shark-tooth pendant on Yasmin's kitchen floor, he phoned me."

"At three in the morning?" Yasmin asked, her eyebrows popping up in surprise.

"Yes, he said he was sure the attacker was Kirk. He asked Pedro and me to give Patterson a ride to Florida." Diego added, "A boat ride," to clarify his comment. "We handed him over to the Sheriff's Department."

Yasmin's mouth dropped open, her latte-colored skin flushing bright pink with anger. "You've been withholding this information since November?" she hoarsely demanded. *When was this stupid cough going to go away?*

"Jesus!" Jessica shouted, "You kidnapped him, and then you made us feel like criminals for not telling you about a few jewels and coins."

Antonio stood up and made calming motions with his hands, "Calm down everyone!" he said, tightly. "We don't want your neighbors investigating the loud voices coming from your house, or calling the local *policía*."

Jessica angrily flipped her hair over her shoulder, glaring at Diego.

"Jess, you're right. We overreacted to your news about the treasure," Diego said, as he reached into the refrigerator and pulled out a cold beer. He twisted the top off, extending the opened bottle to Jessica, "Peace offering?"

Snatching the bottle from his hand, she reached out with her left and gave him a hard open-palmed slap on his shoulder. "Asshole!"

"Ouch," Diego rubbed his arm, adding, "Si, but a *pendejo* who is your devoted friend."

"Lying-*pendejo* friend," Jessica countered with a scowl.

He gave her a little pop on the shoulder, grinning boyishly at her, "Are we good now?"

"Maybe," she grumbled.

Yasmin rubbed her forehead, trying to ease the pain that had settled between her eyes, "We can't continue to just wait and do nothing. There must be something we can do to find Carlos."

Antonio reflexively checked the screen of Yasmin's phone, still laying quietly on the table. "The other building that you mentioned, where is it?"

"It is the abandoned hotel project, the *Unik,*" she said, then added, "near the southwestern side of the island."

"I'm not familiar with that one. How big is it?"

Diego popped one shoulder up in a shrug, then said, "Small hotel, four or five floors, plus roof-top, restaurant, big lobby, and designed for seventy-five luxury apartments. Bigger than the one you checked yesterday."

"Do you know if there is a security guard on that property?" he asked.

"Not that we know of," Pedro responded, "It is surrounded by a rusting wire fence. You'll need a pair of cutters."

"How about we," Antonio indicated himself and the other two men, "take Sparky and search that area tomorrow morning?"

"Sure," Diego agreed, "but what about that message you sent the kidnappers?"

Antonio checked Yasmin's still silent mobile, "If we get a reply that will change our plans. In the meantime, we should try to get some sleep. We are all running on empty."

"That we are," Pedro agreed, puffing out a breath.

"Four-hour shifts?" Diego said to Pedro, referring to their plan to safeguard both Yasmin and Jessica.

"Sure, I'll take the first four," he answered.

"No need," Antonio replied, indicating the sofa, "I'll spend the night here. You guys go home to your own beds."

"Okay good, what time tomorrow?"

Antonio looked at his watch. "It is one-thirty now. Let's sleep a few hours, grab a quick breakfast, and head out at eight."

"Why so late?" Yasmin queried, "Wouldn't sunrise be better?"

Four sets of eyes turned to Antonio, "Yes, and no. Yes, because we might catch the guy or guys napping. And no, because I am hoping that we will be less conspicuous by ambling around the area with the dog, just nosey guys having a look at an idea for a potential investment. Not skulking around."

Yasmin didn't think much of Antonio's idea, but he was an experienced cop so he should know what he was doing. But still, why wait so long?

Jessica listlessly gathered up the food wrappers and stacked the empty take-out boxes, dumping everything in her garbage can.

Antonio gently rolled the antique treasure in the clean tea towel, "I assume, Jessica, that you have a secure location for these?"

"Yes, like Yasmin. It's a personal safe, bolted to the wall in my clothes cupboard," She pointed towards the end of the hallway.

"Okay, let's put this away for now, until we have a better idea of what we are up against."

"Sure," she said, taking the parcel from his hands and walking towards her bedroom, "Are you sure you trust me not to abscond with the loot?"

Chapter 33

January 4th Morning

Diego helped his eldest son, ten-year-old José, with his reading while Cristina bustled around the kitchen preparing an early breakfast for the family. The kids were still on their winter holiday break, and school wouldn't start until after the Day of the Kings, but José was a reluctant scholar. His teacher had assigned extra lessons to be completed over the holidays in an attempt to improve his grades.

Cristina said, "I am so glad you are home, *mi amor.*"

Their home was noisy and filled with laughter. Good smells from Cristina's cooking made Diego's stomach growl loudly, saliva squirting under his tongue in anticipation. He had recently missed many family meals while this unresolved kidnapping situation continued to control their lives. Thinking of Carlos being held captive for going on four days, he felt guilty about the delicious food he was about to eat. He silently offered a heart-felt prayer for his friend's well-being.

"Me too, but I have to go out again soon," Diego replied cryptically, reminding her that the group was planning to search the derelict *Unik* hotel site.

She flicked a worried glance in his direction, "Si, of course, but it is important that the children see you for a few minutes."

"Where are you going, *papi*?" José turned his inquisitive brown eyes to his father.

"I have something to do for *Tio* Carlos, *mi hijo*."

"May I come?" José asked.

Diego rested his large brown hand comfortably over his son's smaller one, "No, son. Another time."

"But you promised me last time that I could come with you."

Uncertain about what he was referring to, Diego looked at José with a question in his eyes, "When did I promise you?"

"A few nights ago, when you said *Tio* Carlos needed you. It was very late at night."

Damn it, now I remember. The call from Yasmin three nights ago. "I'm sorry, José. This is grown-up stuff. I can't take you with me," Diego replied, side-stepping his son's request by repeating a familiar excuse that his father had offered when he didn't want to include him.

The boy's face crumpled, and tears brimmed his eyelashes. He looked down at his school work, avoiding his dad's gaze. Diego knew José's feelings were hurt, but he would rebound quickly. Diego was familiar with the feeling from when he was his son's age, wanting to be a man too soon; his *papi* had gently reminded him that he was just a child, with time to enjoy life before he would be burdened with adult duties.

"Truly, son, I am sorry." He wrapped a strong arm around his son's thin shoulders, pulling him close as he kissed the top of his head. The smell of a small heated body filled his nostrils, not the rank, animal stink of a sweaty man, but the mild tang of an active little boy.

Mutely, José nodded his unhappy acceptance.

Over the top of José's bent head, Cristina smiled knowingly at Diego. Their son was disappointed. It would pass.

Twenty minutes later, Diego pushed away from the table, and lightly rubbed his full stomach. "I can hardly move, I am so full." Rising to hug and kiss his wife, he said, "*Gracias mi amor*, for the delicious breakfast."

"Be careful," she whispered quietly, as he held her close.

"Don't worry," he replied just as quietly. Kissing his younger children, Diego realized José had left the table without excusing himself or saying goodbye. "Say goodbye to José for me please, *mi amor*. I think he is still upset with me."

"I will. He worships you and he hates to be left behind."

"I know, I know. But not this time." Diego patted the front pocket of his jeans. His knife was in its usual spot. Gathering up keys and cellphone, he pecked her one more time on the cheek and waved goodbye to the family.

Stepping to the curb, he pulled open the door of his Jeep and levered his substantial thighs past the steering wheel. The plan was to meet at Jessica's, then thoroughly check the abandoned hotel.

Outside Jessica's *casita*, the street was quiet. It was too early for the out-of-school youngsters to be up, and past the time when most of the adults left for work. It was that funny lull that happened for a brief period in the morning. Yasmin stood beside Jessica, watching while she faced off with Antonio.

With her fists bunched and propped on her slim hips, Jessica said, "It's at least a five-storey building if you count the roof. Yasmin, Sparky, and I can search one floor," she said, pointing at Yasmin and then herself, "and the three of you one floor each. That would just leave the rooftop, and whoever was done first could search there. It would be quicker," she said, arguing quietly.

"Señorita Sanderson, please, don't be difficult," Antonio said.

Oh, oh. Yasmin instinctively glanced at Jessica's face. Now she was pissed-off, to use one of Jessica's favorite Canadianisms. Angry. Livid. Steamed.

"Difficult? I'm being difficult?" Jessica said, her tone low and tight. "We just want to help find our friend."

"*Si*, I understand, but this could be a very dangerous situation." Antonio replied. Yasmin was sure he wanted to add, 'and too dangerous for the little women'.

"We'll be okay, Jess," Diego said amicably, "You and Yasmin have enough on your hands already, what with managing the restaurant and making Yasmin's house liveable again," Diego said. "The three of us and Sparky can easily search the building in a couple of hours. We'll call as soon as we can."

"Fine. Take my dog." She threw her hands in the air, and stomped away.

Yasmin glanced back towards Jessica, then at Antonio. Her eyes flicked to Pedro who was waiting in his truck with his hands resting on the steering wheel. He shrugged. The women weren't going to win this battle.

"Come on, let's get going," said Pedro.

Antonio got in the passenger side, lifting Sparky in with him and placing the dog on the floor at his feet. Pedro pulled in front of Diego's Jeep and headed south. There had been some discussion on whether or not they needed both vehicles, but it never hurt to be prepared for any situation.

As Diego's vehicle started to roll forward, Yasmin's cellphone rang, indicating a call, not a message. She inhaled sharply, holding her hand up, signalling Diego to wait until she answered. "*Si, bueno*?" she tentatively inquired.

"Señorita Yasmin?" a cool feminine voice asked, "Yasmin Medina?"

"Si, this is Yasmin. Who am I speaking to, please?" Yasmin didn't recognize the voice.

She glanced over to Diego as he anxiously mouthed a question, "Kidnapper?"

She shrugged one shoulder and gave him a worried I-don't-know look, while concentrating on the woman's voice.

"This is Elena Hernandez. I called the restaurant looking for Carlos, but they gave me your name and number instead." She added, explaining, "I am a friend of Carlos."

"Oh?" Yasmin answered, "How can I help you Señora Hernandez?" Fingertips bleached white from clutching the mobile tightly, Yasmin exhaled and slightly loosened her death-grip as she tried to sort out why this woman was calling her.

"I am at Carlos' house," Elena said, "and I am worried. It doesn't look like anyone has been here for a few days. The milk has spoiled in his refrigerator and his bed hasn't been slept in."

Thinking the woman was surprisingly familiar with Carlos and his routines, Yasmin answered, "I'm so sorry, Señora Hernandez, Carlos isn't on the island right now."

"Really? But he knew I was coming to Isla. Where is he?" Elena asked.

"His sister, Mariana, has taken ill, and he drove his mother to Mérida to visit with her."

"Mérida? But Mariana lives in Valladolid." Yasmin heard suspicion in the woman voice.

"Yes, but the doctor thought it best if she was in the hospital in Mérida."

"Oh no, what's wrong with our little Mariana?"

Our little Mariana? Who was this woman? Yasmin stumbled a bit with her reply, "I'm not exactly sure. Carlos seemed a bit embarrassed talking about it, so perhaps female problems of some sort?" came her spur-of-the-moment response. "You know how men don't like to talk about stuff like that." She babbled nervously.

"I see, but why doesn't Carlos answer his phone?"

"I think it is a hospital rule that cellphones have to be turned off," Yasmin replied, hoping that would finally appease the inquisitive woman.

"For three days?"

"Oh, well he left the island in a hurry, and he probably forgot to take his charger with him." Yasmin looked helplessly at Diego, pointing at her cellphone clamped to her ear. She silently signalled him, asking what she should do to calm the woman's suspicions. The last thing they needed was someone raising the alarm about Carlos' absence.

Diego tweaked a smile and reached out a large work-roughened hand, taking the cell from Yasmin. "Elena is this you?" he asked, pleasantly.

"Si, this is Elena."

"This is Diego Avalos, Carlos' friend. Do you remember me?"

"Of course, how are you Diego?"

"*Todo bien, gracias*," he replied, putting a smile in his voice, aiming for a friendly tone. "Yasmin's right. Carlos is in Mérida with his mom and sister. He emailed me yesterday to explain he had forgotten his phone charger," Diego lied smoothly. "He thinks he'll be back tomorrow or the next day at the latest."

"Oh, okay. I wish he had told me," she said. "He knew I was coming to Isla this week."

"Again, I'm sorry Elena," Diego said, adding, "Could I get Carlos to call you later in the week?" Diego avoided Yasmin's questioning look.

"Thank you, Diego," said Elena. "I'll be at my mother's house for a few days."

"Please say hello to your mother for me. I'll make sure Carlos calls you as soon as possible," he said, before disconnecting the call.

Diego handed the device to Yasmin with a wink. "It's a guy thing," he said.

"Fine, but who is she?" Yasmin asked, her eyebrows scrunched over her deep green eyes. "And why does she have a key to Carlos' house?"

"Ah, well," Diego hesitated, "that was the former Señora Mendoza, Carlos' ex-wife. I guess he never got around to changing the locks."

He waved sheepishly and drove away, leaving Yasmin standing on the street with a shocked expression on her face.

Chapter 34

January 4th Morning

Setting his feet on the floor, Patterson stood, leaving the empty hammock to swing behind him. He stretched. After four days of living rough in the vacant hotel, he smelled like a dumpster-diver. Picking up Mendoza's phone, Kirk inserted the battery and turned it on. Even with so little use, the screen showed low battery status. Maybe he could buy a cheap charger at the internet store in *Centro*, and make a deal with the nearby pizza place to recharge the phone while he lingered over a cup of coffee or a beer.

He quickly checked for messages. There were several missed calls from a number identified as Elena, whoever that was. And there was one short text from that bitch Yasmin's number—*Where? When?* Good, now he had her trying to contact him. She could wait until he was good and ready to respond. He powered off the phone, removed the battery to prevent anyone from tracking the phone, and tucked everything into his side pockets.

Disgusted at his stench, he decided to go for an early morning swim, and quietly crept down the bank. There were several construction workers building a new house a few lots south, but there was nothing that directly overlooked his hiding spot. He picked his way to the shoreline, past smashed pieces of plywood, lumber bristling with nails, and hardened concrete spills—rubble discarded years ago when the building was under construction. He stripped off his foul clothes and plunged into the warm ocean. Fifteen minutes later he reluctantly pulled on the same fetid shorts and shirt and trekked back towards the hotel lobby.

Diego drove to the neighborhood of the unfinished hotel project. Turning the Jeep onto a rough dirt road, he stashed the recognizable vehicle deep in the bushes. He winced when the thin branches screeched along the passenger side, scoring the shiny black paint. He looked around for the white Nissan truck but couldn't spot it, so he thought Pedro had likely hidden his vehicle too.

Pulling himself out of the vehicle, Diego shut the driver's door, leaving it unlocked. He wanted quick access just in case they had to make a hasty departure. He reflexively patted his pocket once again, confirming that he had his knife.

Hearing the soft shuffle of footsteps behind him, Diego turned to see Pedro, Antonio and Sparky walking towards him on the narrow gravel lane. The dog was wearing his harness and Antonio held the end of his leash. It was a condition set by Jess, 'you take my dog, you use his harness'. From previous conversations, Diego knew she was paranoid that the pooch would get hit by a car. It was probably a fair concern, since judging by Sparky's habit of running on three legs with one back leg tucked up when he was tired, he had been hit by a car at some point before Jessica had adopted the little guy. A small dog on a dark road didn't usually fare well when it came in contact with a fast-moving vehicle.

"What took you so long?" Antonio asked. "Did Señorita Sanderson give you another earful after we left?"

"No," Diego replied with a big grin that displayed his well-cared-for teeth. "Yasmin got a call from Carlos' ex-wife, Elena, just as I was about to leave," he said.

"Elena? I haven't seen her in years. I wonder if she is still knock-em-dead gorgeous," Pedro mused. "What did she want?"

"She said she was visiting her mom," Diego replied, "But she still has a key to Carlos' house and she discovered he hasn't been home recently."

"Oh, that's not good, on so many levels."

"No kidding. Carlos missing, ex-wife snooping, and Yasmin wondering what the hell's going on." Diego said with a little chuckle, "I had to do a little creative story telling. I think I have it sorted for the moment, *mas o menos*." He said, tilting his hand back and forth in a 'more or less' gesture.

"Ex-wife with a key to the house? That could be tense." Antonio said with a grin, then motioned towards Sparky. "He's interested in something."

The dog was investigating the back of Diego's Jeep, stuffing his nose tightly against the bottom of the door and inhaling deeply.

Sparky turned his questioning brown eyes towards Diego, his eyebrows dancing up and down.

"What's up, boy?" Diego asked. Using his hand to shade the glare on the glass, he peered through the darkly tinted rear window. "There's nothing there."

Pedro waved a dismissive hand, "Don't worry about it. This guy has a super sensitive nose. A bitch in heat probably walked by your vehicle this morning and he can still smell her scent."

Diego chuckled, "Yeah probably." He cast a distracted glance at the auto, asking, "Everyone ready then?"

Antonio reached down and fingered Sparky's collar. It had two metal tags that clinked softly when the dog moved. "No sense giving the bad guys a warning," he said as he unlatched the collar and jammed it deep into his left pocket. Once we are in position, I'll let him roam free to search for smells he might recognize."

"Okay, let's do this."

Chapter 35

January 4th Morning

Motionless on the floor behind the driver's seat, José held his breath when he heard the dog sniffing. José was covered by a large blanket his dad kept in the Jeep for emergencies or for his baby brother's naps. He silently prayed his *papi* wouldn't look inside to see what was so interesting to Sparky.

Hearing the stranger say "Let's do this," José quietly released his breath.

Waiting until he could no longer hear the men's footsteps, José cracked open the passenger door and peered out. He tentatively set one sneakered foot on the ground, then the other, and gently pushed the door shut until it clicked. It was latched but not fully closed. Shutting it properly would be too noisy, and daddy might turn around to see who was messing with his vehicle.

José was worried *papi* would be angry with him for hiding in the car and for following the men. But a few months before, when he had done something similar, his daddy had scolded him briefly then laughed, and tousled his dark curly hair—calling him *his little man*. José had skipped his hated school lessons and snuck into the Jeep, then crept on board the *Sea Witch,* hiding until the boat was well out to sea. As punishment for worrying his mama, he had to wash the family supper dishes for a whole week, all by himself, but it was worth it to escape a full day of school and to spend time fishing with his dad and *Tio* Pedro.

José thought of himself as an amateur detective. He would often find lost items for his mom, things she had left in an unusual location or that one of the younger kids had used and not properly replaced. He liked to solve mysteries. His dad and friends were acting very strangely.

Late last night his parents had whispered about *papi* searching the big building near Punta Sur with *Tio* Pedro and the policeman from Mexico City. He didn't know why, but for some reason they were worried that *Tio* Carlos was inside the building. It was a scary place, but if the men were going to search, then he wanted to help.

José hid behind a bushy plant by the side of the road, checking both directions for vehicles, then he scampered across and disappeared into the tangled foliage. He crept along the stone wall, wary of scorpions and snakes, and eased around the corner looking for a way inside the wire fence. Testing the strands with his hand, he finally located a spot where the wire mesh had been cut, the bright ends glinting in the morning sun.

Looking at the crushed vegetation underfoot, he whispered to himself, "This is where they went in." Squeezing his slender frame through the gap, he carefully straightened the wire, camouflaging the entrance enough to fool a quick look.

José flitted from one shadowed area to another listening for clues as to where his *papi* and his *Tio* Pedro had gone. The main entrance was a wide-open area with marble floors covered by blown debris and thick-stemmed vines. He carefully stepped around the areas where scorpions could be lurking. Dropped in the middle of the expanse were five enormous crates stamped with the word *elevadores*, elevators for the empty hotel. The open shafts leading to the upper floors were crudely boarded over. José could hear pigeons, or maybe Inca doves, cooing in the dark recesses of the building. Particles circled in the filtered sunlight as his footsteps disturbed the thick layer of sand and road dust. This was a lot scarier than sneaking on his *papi's* boat.

At either end of the main floor were two stairways. Unsure which way he should go, José chose the right-hand set of steps. He breathed a small sigh of relief when he noticed footprints on the stairs. The shoe print of one set was similar to the pattern his dad's sandals made. He also noticed what looked like drag marks in the dust, as if something heavy had been tugged upwards, one stair at a time. Unsure what that could be, Jose quietly positioned his foot on the first step, listening for clues as to where the men had gone.

About to enter the building from an ocean-side entrance, Patterson heard the light sound of a shoe chafing against rough concrete. He froze in place. Listening intently, he popped his mouth open a little, a trick that according to his recent cellmate was supposed to sharpen the sense of hearing. Another light step. *A kid exploring the building? Maybe.*

Hugging the concrete wall, Patterson slowly eased his head around the entryway, scanning for threats in either direction. He saw a slight figure, a young boy of probably no more than nine or ten years old, disappearing up the stairway on the opposite side of the lobby. Silently picking his way across the littered floor, Kirk stopped at the bottom step and listened. The boy was climbing the stairs, probably headed to the rooftop. A nosey kid was a problem. Judging by the number of empty beer cans and discarded candy wrappers, the never-finished building drew young kids and teenagers looking for a spot to hang out for a few hours away from the prying eyes of parents. This stupid little punk was going to mess up his plans.

Silently and swiftly, Patterson ascended the stairway. Just as the kid reached the entrance to the third floor, Kirk reached out with his right hand and clamped on to the boy's thin arm.

"Hey!" the boy yelled, his voice squeaky with fear. "You're hurting me."

Patterson glared at the kid, hoping to scare him into leaving without discovering that Mendoza was handcuffed in a nearby room. "I'm the security guard for this building. You need to leave."

"Who's out there?" came a hoarse but recognizable shout from the next room.

Patterson clamped his left hand over the boy's mouth, hissing in his ear, "Keep quiet."

The boy snapped his teeth closed, biting hard.

"You little bastard!" shouted Patterson as he reflexively pulled his hand away. "You bit me!" Thin arms flailed at Patterson's face; the boy's sneakers kicked ineffectually at his shin.

"*Tio* Carlos! It's me, José! Help! *¡Ayúdame!*"

"Sonofabitch!" Patterson yelled.

"José, run, get away!" Carlos shouted.

Patterson scrambled to pull his stiletto from his pocket with one hand, as he forced José's left arm up behind his shoulders in a police maneuver. "Stupid move, kid," Kirk snarled, pressing the knife blade under the boy's chin. "Don't make another sound or I'll kill you. You hear me?"

Afraid to nod his head in understanding, José blinked his eyes. Tears cascaded down his cheeks as he stared wide-eyed in terror at his captor.

Chapter 36

January 4th Morning

On the second floor of the building, Diego stared at a cheap blue nylon hammock strung between two walls of the bare room. Someone had recently used the area as their living space. The rough concrete floor was littered with discarded plastic bottles and food wrappers. A small pile of windblown refuse had collected in one corner of the room. His head snapped back as he heard a young, fear-filled voice yell.

"*Tio* Carlos! It's me, José! Help! *¡Ayúdame!*"

"*Madre de Dios*, José!" Diego ran to the stairway and bellowed as loudly as an enraged elephant, "Pedro. Upstairs. My son is here. He needs help!"

"What the hell?" Pedro responded, charging up the stairway from the first floor towards the roar of Diego's voice and his brother-in-law's thumping footsteps.

The two large men burst into the third-floor hallway within seconds of each other. They quickly scanned for any sign of the boy. The open-air space was empty.

"José!" Diego yelled, "It's *papi*. Where are you?" He spun in place, checking all of the visible exits, waiting for his son to call out. Every muscle was taut with anger, his body pumping adrenaline and blood at maximum capacity. His breathing was slow and deep as he willed himself to listen intently for the scrape of a shoe, the clink of metal, the snuffle of a child. Anything. *Where are you, son?*

"Guys, in here!" yelled a ragged and familiar voice.

"Carlos?" Pedro stuck his head through the open entry, "Hey, man, I'm glad to see you."

Half-aware that Pedro was talking to Carlos, Diego concentrated on listening for his son. "Likewise," he heard Carlos say, then, "Patterson has José. It sounds like he is on the other side of the hotel but on this floor."

"One second." Pedro turned and shouted towards Diego, "I've got Carlos, not José. Try the other side."

Cold fear flooded his veins. Diego pounded in the other direction without a backward glance. Carlos would be okay; he was sick with worry about José.

Pedro's eyes restlessly scanned the room as he strode towards Carlos.

Carlos held up his hands. "Got your knife?"

"Always." Pedro knelt on the concrete in front of Carlos and probed in the keyhole of the metal cuffs. "Whoof, you stink," he said wrinkling his nose in distaste.

"These aren't exactly luxury accommodations," Carlos replied with a grim smile on his face.

"No kidding." As the mechanism released and one of the links fell free, Pedro flicked a glance at Carlos' dog-tired eyes, "You okay?"

"I think so." He gingerly touched the blood crusted scab with his free hand. "Maybe a small concussion, I'm not sure."

Pedro clicked open the remaining link, and stood. He gripped Carlos' forearm as his friend steadied himself, placing the palm of his left hand on the wall and slowly pulling himself erect.

"Patterson is probably hiding somewhere in the building," Carlos said, leaning against the wall as he cautiously rubbed his battered wrists. His fingers tingled with the sudden increase in circulation. "Go help Diego," he said. "I'll catch up in a couple of minutes."

Pedro nodded, "Yeah, okay. But take it easy. No heroics." Moving swiftly towards the other side of the hotel, Pedro added, "Antonio is somewhere in the building with Sparky."

"Good," he said to Pedro's back as he disappeared through the doorway.

Chapter 37

January 4th Morning

Sparky barked once loudly. He glanced up at Antonio and then switched his gaze to stare intently at the staircase.

Antonio stilled his breathing and listened, closely watching the dog's reaction. He and Sparky had been searching the rooftop for signs of either the kidnappers or Carlos when they heard the loud voices. Pedro was on the first floor and Diego the second. He had decided to start at the top with Sparky and work his way down to the other floors.

"Come on boy, let's see what's going on." Antonio bent down and removed Sparky's harness, dropping it and his leash onto the rooftop. He could retrieve it later. Reaching for his weapon, Antonio followed the dog as he sped down the stairs. The only sound was the clicking of Sparky's nails on the concrete and a murmur of an indistinct conversation. Unable to clearly hear the words or identify the voices, Antonio held his gun at shoulder height, barrel pointing towards the roof.

A deep growl rumbled out of Sparky's throat as he skidded to a stop at the bottom of the stairway. Antonio slammed his left arm against the wall to stop his forward momentum, swinging the pistol into a shooting stance as he poked his head around the doorway. A quick glimpse—a tall thin gringo holding a knife under the chin of a small boy. Patterson and José. Antonio ducked his head back.

"Police!" Antonio yelled. "I've got a gun. Release the boy." He moved slowly and smoothly back into view and aimed at the center of the man's chest. "Let him go."

"Two big scary guys and only one gun between the both of you." Kirk smirked, as he dragged José closer to the sheer edge of a third-floor terrace.

"Backup is on the way," Antonio lied.

"Sure it is," Kirk said, quickly glancing down. It was a three-story drop to a sloping bank that angled towards the ocean. The ground was littered with the discarded construction materials that he had recently picked his way through to gain access to the ocean. "I've got the kid. You shoot me, and we'll both drop over the edge."

"Antonio, don't shoot," Diego pleaded, his voice thick with emotion.

Without moving his head, Antonio focused briefly on Diego. He was about fifteen feet away, staring helplessly at his son. Antonio refocused on Patterson. "Okay, now what?"

"Put the gun on the floor and slide it over to me."

"Not going to happen."

Patterson pressed on the knife, "Then I'll cut his throat, like I should have done to that bitch, Yasmin," he sneered.

"Antonio, do as he says."

Antonio glanced at Diego. He saw the man's eyes frantically ping-ponging between his son and Patterson.

"Yeah, Antonio, listen to your buddy." Patterson moved the knife an inch, breaking the surface of the boy's skin, releasing a small trickle of blood. "One quick swipe and it's all over for the kid."

"Leave the kid alone!" Antonio shouted. He fumbled with the gun, pretending his hands were shaking, as he allowed his eyes to briefly scan the room. Hidden in a small alcove, Pedro pushed himself tight against the wall. He was much closer to Patterson and José. Antonio saw Pedro briefly nod, indicating he was ready. No sign of Carlos, but he could be anywhere in the building. Sparky had slowly inched to the outside of the room, head down and tail flat on the floor. Was the dog frightened of Patterson?

This wasn't a good situation. The moment Patterson got his hands on the gun they were dead men. With both hands up in the surrender position, Antonio crouched on one knee and lowered the pistol to the floor, giving it a small shove that moved the weapon five feet.

"Cute," Patterson said. "Now give it a kick, hotshot, so that it reaches me but doesn't go over the edge."

Martinez stepped closer to the weapon. Pulling his right foot back in a soft kick, he knocked it further across the room.

"Jesus, I thought all wetbacks were soccer players. You kick like a girl."

"Football players," Antonio automatically corrected. Keeping his eyes aimed at Kirk, he used his peripheral vision to check Diego and Pedro. "We say football. Americans say soccer."

"Whatever." Kirk flicked a glance at the gun, then suddenly he pounced. As he reached to grab the weapon, his knife moved away from the boy's throat.

A silent cyclone of white and brown sprang forward. Sparky closed his trap-like jaws on Patterson's right wrist. With a howl of rage and pain, Kirk attempted to jerk the animal loose using his left hand. The dog hung on.

Antonio yanked up his right pant leg and drew his smaller back-up weapon, searching for a clear line of sight.

Pedro lunged for José, wrapping him tightly in his arms and pulling the boy's face tight against his chest as they rolled across the floor and banged against an adjoining wall.

Sparky clamped his jaw harder, forcing his teeth deeper. Patterson attempted to turn the knife into the animal's chest, but his hand was slick with blood and the knife clattered to the floor. He desperately swung his foot towards the dog's head.

As Kirk lifted his foot to boot Sparky in the head, Carlos dove across the floor like a baseball player skidding into home plate. He scooped up the Glock, aimed it at Kirk's chest and squeezed the trigger. The weapon didn't fire.

Antonio had his chance; he fired a burst of three bullets. The force of the bullets knocked Kirk backwards towards the rim, tearing his hand free from Sparky's grip.

Diego strode rapidly across the room and punted the unconscious Patterson over the edge, then stared at the dropping body. His chest heaved with deep breaths; the veins in his neck were the size of thick cables.

In a frozen tableau of men, dog, and boy, no one moved. Dust motes circled in the warm air, birds twittered, and palm trees swayed in the light breeze. A few seconds later, the meaty thump of a body hitting something unyielding echoed though the hotel.

"What the hell just happened?" Carlos asked, breathing hard. He sat on the floor with his forearms propped on his knees, the un-fired Glock dangling from his right hand.

Chapter 38

January 4th Morning

"We just created a whole lot of paperwork, is what happened," Antonio said as he peered over the edge, checking that Patterson hadn't somehow miraculously survived three gunshots and a thirty-foot drop. He appeared to be dead. Turning to grin at Carlos, he added, "Good to see you, *hermano*."

"I'm glad to see you too. Very glad." Favoring his left knee, Carlos limped over to Antonio, passing him the gun handle first. "Why didn't it fire?"

Momentarily ignoring the question, Antonio wrapped his arm around Carlos' shoulder, preparing to guy-hug him, but backed off when he saw Carlos wince. "Sore ribs?"

"Yeah, he booted me a few times when we were getting to know each other."

"We evened up the score for you," Antonio said quietly as he held a finger to his lips, then pointed towards José still tucked against Pedro's chest.

Nodding his understanding, Carlos answered in a near whisper as he stared at the unmoving body. "His head is at a funny angle."

Antonio grunted, "Yeah, I noticed that."

Pointing at the weapon, Carlos said, "It scared the hell out of me when it wouldn't fire."

"You probably didn't get a good enough grip when you grabbed it. You have to put your finger all the way over the trigger to bypass the safety system." Antonio holstered the gun, then bent and tucked the smaller pistol in his ankle holster.

"Thank god you had the backup piece."

"Always. I don't go anywhere without at least two. Cops like guns, lots of guns," Antonio said, his face breaking out in a big white-toothed grin. He looked to the other side of the room where Pedro was untangling himself from José's limbs. He had kept the boy's face buried in his chest, preventing José from seeing Patterson die. Good move on his part. "Pedro," he said, pointing at his own elbows and knees, then at Pedro, "You're bleeding."

Pedro nodded. He checked José for injuries, then passed the sobbing child to his dad, before looking at his own wounds.

Diego squatted and fiercely hugged his ten-year-old son, too relieved to scold the boy. "What are you doing here, *hijo*?"

José hiccoughed, then wiped a hand under his snotty nose, "I wanted to help you, *papi*," he wailed.

"Your mother is going to be very unhappy with both of us," Diego sighed, sharing a knowing look with Carlos. José snuggled against Diego's broad chest, clutching his dad's shirt with his sticky fists.

Worn-out, dirty, thinner than a few days ago, Carlos grinned at Diego, mouthing *thank you*. His friend nodded, a weary smile creasing his face.

"I'm sorry for causing trouble," José snuffled, wiping his nose again and smearing the goo on his shorts.

"It's okay, son, we'll figure things out." Diego drew the boy farther away from the rim of the terrace. "Just stay over here; don't go near the edge."

Antonio smiled warmly as he walked towards José. The poor little kid looked scared to death. "Hey, *hombre*. You were a real brave guy." He held up his closed hand, gesturing for a man-to-man fist-bump. The boy complied, shyly peering at him. "I'm a friend of your *papi*'s," Antonio said, deliberately not mentioning his own name. "Can I have a look at your chin?" he asked, studying the boy's face.

José glanced up at his dad, who nodded in agreement. "Okay," he said timidly.

Antonio carefully tilted the boy's head up, inspecting the cut. Thankfully it was more of a scrape than an actual cut. It would heal with no physical reminder of today. But how would the boy cope mentally with the circumstances? That was something that would have to be closely watched. Antonio smiled reassuringly at Diego, "He's a good kid."

Diego nodded, smiling down at his son's tear-stained face. "Yes, a good kid who is going to be helping *Mama* with household chores for a long time. A very long time."

José nodded mutely in agreement.

"You ready to get back to work?" Pedro pulled Carlos into a bear hug, causing him to inhale sharply, "You've had four days of rest and relaxation while your staff has been slaving away at the restaurant."

"Take it easy on my ribs, *hermano*." Carlos snorted a weary laugh, "I want to phone my family and Yasmin, tell them I'm okay." He glanced towards the terrace edge. "I think my phone went over the side." Holding out his hand he asked Pedro, "Can I use yours?"

"Sure, but let's talk about this for a few minutes with Antonio before we make any phone calls," Pedro suggested in a low voice.

Antonio grunted a quiet laugh, adding, "We'll stick to the truth, mostly. Carlos was kidnapped by an international felon. Sparky helped us find Carlos. The guy threatened to kill Carlos. I shot the kidnapper. He fell over the side." He brushed his hands together. "End of story."

Standing across the room, Diego discreetly pointed his chin towards his son, mouthing, "What about him?"

Antonio shook his head, "Just you, me, Pedro, and Carlos. And Sparky. It's easier that way." He locked his gaze on Diego.

Diego nodded in agreement. *Kicking a wounded man off the third floor of the building hadn't been a great idea, but Patterson had threatened to kill his son, and his rage had overridden his reasoning.* Diego gently laid his hands on his son's shoulders, looking José in the eye. "You understand, *hijo*? You and I now share a grownup secret, man-to-man. You must never tell anyone that you were here."

"*Si papi*. I understand," he nodded solemnly. "What should I tell *mamá*? My clothes are very dirty, and she will be unhappy."

"Leave that to me, *hijo*. I'll talk to her," Diego said, hoping he could explain the situation to Cristina. She was going to be one angry mama bear. When he put himself in a dangerous situation it wasn't nearly as problematic for her as one of her babies being in danger. Nothing mattered as much as her kids. Things were about to get interesting at home.

"I want to take José home first and then be here when you notify the policía," said Diego. "Give me fifteen or twenty minutes."

"Sure, take your time," Antonio said, "We won't call this in until you get back."

"Maybe we should check on Patterson just to be sure," Pedro said, disinterest obvious in the tone of his voice.

"Okay," Antonio said, "I'll check for a pulse." Antonio beckoned Carlos, "Can you watch him until I get there?" He pointed at the motionless body below, "This guy has had amazing luck at surviving bad situations."

Carlos glanced at Patterson's body, "I don't think we have to worry, but I will keep an eye on him until you signal."

Sparky danced around the men's feet. He excitedly wagged his tail, side to side, around in circles, up and down, and then propeller mode again.

"Are you coming with me?" Antonio asked as he pulled Sparky's collar out of his pocket and bent to fasten it around his neck. "You are one of the guys now, Sparky."

Chapter 39

January 4th Early afternoon

Resting with his elbows on his bent knees, his chin propped on one fist, Carlos stoically watched the flurry of activity surrounding the construction site.

He desperately wanted to scour his body in a hot shower, put on fresh clothes, and toss everything he was wearing into the garbage can. Next, he'd drink a couple of cold beers and wolf down some food. Then he planned to hug Yasmin and fall dead asleep for at least twenty-four hours.

Instead he was dawdling on the stone entrance steps, sharing a bottle of tepid water with a dog, and swatting at the flies that had been drawn by the scent of death. He and the guys waited as the assortment of officials processed the scene and took their statements. He was hoping for the go-ahead to leave.

The first to arrive were six municipal police officers crammed into a black pickup, two in the front and four sitting on a metal bench bolted to the bed of the cargo box. Then the municipal Comandante de Policía was notified because the death involved a foreigner.

Next, the contingent of State Police officers based on Isla Mujeres were summoned to the scene. The deceased person was a supposedly-dead American prisoner who had been jailed for multiple rapes and suspected of several murders. The escapee was now certainly dead, killed by an off-duty Policía Federal de Mexico.

The mess was getting more and more complex by the moment. Carlos was relieved that Antonio had excluded ten-year-old José from his statement. Diego would need to take special care to ensure his son didn't suffer nightmares and post-traumatic stress. It wasn't the boy's fault the man had been killed, but he might not fully understand the situation without professional help.

Then the doctor from the hospital arrived and pronounced Patterson dead at the scene.

A group of police trailed their commander while everyone inspected the third-floor space where Patterson was shot, then where Carlos was held captive for four days, and finally the area where Patterson had been living on the second floor. One of the young patrolmen had picked up Sparky's leash and harness from the roof. Carrying it down to the main entrance, he had handed the gear to Carlos.

Antonio surrendered both of his pistols to the State Police. The ranking officer did a quick sniff test of the Glock 17's barrel, and passed the gun back. Carlos couldn't hear the words but he saw the man nod in agreement. The handgun hadn't been discharged, so there was no need to seize the weapon. Antonio would have felt completely naked without at least one weapon affixed to his body.

Carlos' broken and unusable iPhone had been found in Patterson's pocket by the doctor. His Rolex watch was back on his left wrist, and his wallet was tucked into his right front pocket. Both had been uncovered on the second floor under a small pile of refuse, Patterson's makeshift hiding place for valuables. His bank and credit cards were still in the wallet. He knew his two thousand pesos had been taken by Patterson a few days ago.

Carlos turned to Pedro, "Can I use your phone?" Pedro handed his mobile over without raising his head from his position on the floor.

Flicking a finger across the screen, Carlos activated the smartphone. He thumbed in his dad's number from memory and pressed the device to his ear. While he waited for the number to connect, he scratched the top of Sparky's head and massaged his ears. The dog's tongue lolled out, dripping saliva. "You need another drink of water?" Carlos asked him, but Sparky didn't answer. He just leaned into Carlos, happy for the attention.

Finally, Carlos heard his dad's voice in his ear, "Si bueno?"

"Hola *papa*, it's me, Carlos."

"Carlos! Where are you? Are you okay?" His father exclaimed, "Lupe, it's Carlos!"

He could hear his mother's strained breathing as she took the cell phone from her husband's hand. "Carlos, *mi amor*, are you alright?" Lupe Mendoza asked.

Hearing the tremble in his mother's voice pinched his heart. His escapades over the years had worried her too many times to count.

"*Si*, I'm okay. I'll see you soon."

"But, we are still in Valladolid," she replied. Carlos could hear the frustration in her voice. "Diego asked us to leave the island for a few days."

"*Si*, I know. Don't worry, I will be a few more hours. I have some things to tidy up with the *policía*." Carlos glanced over at the activity in the fenced courtyard.

"The *policía*! Are you okay, *hijo*?" Lupe's voice sounded frantic.

"I'm fine. They just want to be clear on what happened," he said, gazing around at the anthill of officials snapping photos and scribbling notes.

"We'll be there as soon as we can, *mi amor*," his mother said.

"There's no hurry, take your time." He smiled at that idea; she would be packing her suitcase as soon as he ended this call, pushing his dad to drive her back to Isla as soon as humanly possible. She probably wouldn't wait for the infrequent car ferry, demanding instead that they leave the family car at the Ultramar parking lot and take one of the passenger boats, scheduled to depart every thirty minutes.

"Raúl!"

Carlos grimaced and pulled the phone away from his ear. His mom's voice was loud and crammed with authority when she wanted something done, and done now.

"*Mamá*, I'm fine, honestly," he said, hoping to reassure her, "I'll tell you all about it when I see you." Unseen by Lupe, her son made patting motions with his free hand. It was a reflex action whenever he spoke to her. Worry and exhaustion could trigger atrial fibrillation in her aging heart. "Take it easy *mamá*, everything is fine."

Saying goodbye to his mom and then his dad, Carlos dialed Yasmin's number.

Chapter 40

January 4th Early afternoon

"Carlos," Yasmin whispered, worried the staff might overhear her conversation. "*Mi amor*, are you okay?" she asked, the urgency in her voice unmistakable.

Bemused, Carlos chuckled lightly. This conversation sounded like a repeat of the one with his mother. "*Si*, I'm okay, *carina*," he answered. "Are you at the *Loco Lobo*?"

"Yes. Everything is fine here," she said, quickly adding, "Where are you? I'll come and get you."

"Thank you, but not yet, Yassy, I'm still busy with the *policía*."

"Did you get the guys that did this?"

"You could say that," Carlos hedged. "One guy. Kirk Patterson."

"Kirk." Her voice hardened, "So, he didn't die in Florida."

Carlos flicked his gaze towards the blue plastic tarp covering a mound. "No, but he's dead now."

"Thank God. I hate that man," she said, her fear heating her words. "Are you hurt, *mi amor*? Her voice was softer, concerned.

"Only a little bump on the head," he said, glancing at his battered body. His wrists were blood-encrusted from his attempts to yank the handcuffs free of the pipe. He had at least two cracked ribs, from being repeatedly kicked. Poking through the ragged holes in his black pants, his knees were raw and bleeding—a reward for his useless heroics, diving for the pistol on the rough concrete floor. His left hand explored his right elbow, encountering a sticky wetness. He checked his fingers—blood—okay, maybe a little bit more than a bump on the head.

"It's so good to hear your voice," Yasmin murmured.

He smiled, "I am very happy to hear your voice, *mi amor*."

"Everyone has been worried sick about you."

His eyebrows pinched together, "Who else knows I was kidnapped?"

"Your family, Jessica, the guys, and me," Yasmin whispered warily.

"We need to keep this as quiet as possible, Yasmin." If the drug cartels thought he was a soft target, it could lead to bigger problems, much bigger problems. The cartels were known to kidnap business owners for ransom and not release the victim. Hearing his sharp tone, he attempted to soften his voice. He added with a quiet chuckle, "It's embarrassing to be overpowered by just one guy. Doesn't do much for my tough-guy image."

"Just like a man, worried about your image," her voice was lighter, filled with amusement. "Have you talked to your family yet?"

"Si, I spoke to my parents. They will be returning from Valladolid later today."

"Your mom must have been so happy to hear from you."

"*Si*, she was."

"Are the guys and Sparky with you?"

"Yes, they're all here, and they're okay," Carlos replied.

"Are you sure I can't bring some food, water? Anything?"

"Not right now, Yassy. I'll phone you as soon as we are done here," he said. As he noticed a tall grey-haired man striding towards him, he added, "I have to go. I see the police *jefe* headed this way."

"Oh, wait, before I forget," Yasmin said, "A woman named Elena Hernandez called me. She was looking for you."

"Elena called you?" Carlos said, thinking, *Oh shit! Elena*.

"*Si*, the staff gave her my name and phone number."

"I see. Okay, thanks. I'll call her later in the week." Carlos replied, trying to sound nonchalant about his ex-wife calling his girlfriend. Maybe someone at the restaurant was deliberately trying to stir up trouble. Something to think about.

Saying goodbye and promising again to call as soon as they were cleared to leave, Carlos disconnected.

Pedro reached out a hand, reclaiming his phone. "So, I guess by the expression on your face, Yasmin just told you that Elena is on the island?"

"You knew?"

"Diego was there when Yasmin got the phone call."

"And?"

"She was inside your house and noticed that you hadn't been home for a bit. Diego gave her the same story we have been telling everyone else, about you being in Mérida." Pedro grinned, "She plans to be on the island for about a week."

Exasperated, Carlos blew out a big puff of air, "Great, just what I need. An ex-wife stalking me and my new girlfriend. Just freaking great."

"It might be time to change your locks, lover boy." Antonio quipped, an amused grin crinkling his face.

Carlos felt Sparky tense up, and then stand. Maybe it was just the stern demeanor of the Comandante as he strode in their direction that was unsettling the dog, but after his earlier performance, Carlos was worried that the dog might consider the *jefe* a threat and attack him too. He wrapped the fingers of one hand around the dog's collar, lightly but securely hanging on to him.

"Exactly how do you plan to keep this quiet? The newspaper and television reports monitor the police radios."

Pulling himself into a sitting position, Pedro looked around. "I'm surprised they haven't swarmed this area already."

Carlos pointed at Antonio, "I'm counting on his status as a big-city super-cop to at least keep my name out of the news. The rest of you troublemakers are on your own." Carlos said, laughter crinkling his grimy face.

"Super-cop, I like that," Antonio said, dusting off his trousers and straightening his shirt. He patted his thick black hair, checking that it was still neatly gelled in place. "Show time," he said, clamping his mouth in a firm expression.

Perched on the stone steps of the unfinished lobby, Carlos, Diego, and Pedro watched the body language between the two men, their emphatic gestures and head shakes. Words were spoken with authority, but not loud enough for the subordinates to overhear the conversation.

Carlos remarked, "Antonio seems to be winning the argument."

"Quite the display of testosterone," Pedro said, "but I think the status of a Federal cop trumps that of a State cop."

Diego nodded his chin towards the arguing men, "Looks like our guy won this round." Antonio was smiling as he shook the hand of the older officer. He clapped him on the shoulder like they were new best friends, then turned towards the group waiting on the steps.

Martinez flashed a discrete thumbs up and winked. "We're good to go. The State Police are taking full credit for finding the dangerous American killer who is also considered a person of interest in several deaths, including two Sheriff's Deputies and a transport truck driver. The State Police responded to an anonymous tip from someone who recognized him entering and exiting this abandoned development. The fugitive unfortunately slipped and plunged over the side of the hotel while he was trying to avoid recapture."

"That's it?" Diego queried, his eyebrows popping up in surprise.

"And, I promised a tour of our building the next time he is in Mexico City, with an introduction to my boss. The Comandante would like to work for the Federal Policía." Antonio rolled his eyes.

"Then let's go before the very nice Comandante changes his mind," Carlos said.

Diego pointed to the gravel road across the street. "My vehicle is over there. I'll give you and Sparky a ride," Diego held his nose, "although he smells a lot better than you. You stink like a dog that's rolled in fresh horse crap."

Chapter 41

January 4th Late afternoon

The hot water beat down on Carlos, scalding his scrapes and bruises. It felt good, so good to be clean. He tentatively soaped his hair, avoiding the still painful bump at the back of his head. Diego had urged him get checked at the hospital, but he'd refused, saying he didn't want to answer awkward questions.

Stepping out of the shower, Carlos looked in the mirror. The pupils of his deep brown eyes matched in size and responded quickly when he tested them with the beam of a small flashlight. He knew, from previous bumps on the head, if his pupils were unequal or slow to respond it could indicate a concussion. His looked normal.

Pedro and Antonio had stopped at a *taqueria* on the way to Carlos' place, buying two dozen *res* and *pollo* tacos, several bottles of water, and two dozen *cervezas*. Carlos rapidly scarfed down two meat tacos, followed by a big bottle of water, before heading to the shower. Now, with a towel snugged around his trim waist, he gathered up his filthy torn clothes. He limped into the kitchen and rummaged under the sink until he found a large plastic garbage bag, then unceremoniously dumped his pricey clothes and shoes into the sack. Tying a knot in the top of the bag, he carried it to his back steps and jammed everything in the garbage can. Designer labels be damned. He wasn't wearing those clothes again, ever.

Back in the kitchen area, Carlos opened the refrigerator, searching for a cold beer. Twisting off the top, he up-ended the *cerveza*, rapidly chugging it down, then wiped his mouth with the back of his hand. Scooping up another taco, he chomped it down in three big bites. He patted his flat stomach, burping with the sudden glut of food.

"Thanks for the food, I'm starting to feel human again," he said.

"You're welcome." Antonio glanced over, "You might want to put some clothes on, lover boy. Yasmin phoned while you were in the shower. She's on her way."

Pedro cut in, "Don't bother. You'll just be ripping them off again." He pointed at the towel, "It's quicker this way."

Carlos started to shake his head, the pain reminding him—not a good idea. "No *chucka-chucka* today. I'm too beat up."

Diego levered himself out of Carlos' comfortable, man-sized chair. He gathered up the food wrappers and empty beer bottles, tossing the refuse into the garbage can on top of Carlos' discarded clothes. "I have to get home. Cristina is frantic to find out what happened today. It isn't going to be pretty. I've got a lot of explaining to do about José." He looked hopefully at Antonio. "Come with me? You could use your super-cop abilities on her."

"No," Antonio said. "I don't want to diminish my powers with over-use. You are on your own, *hermano*."

"*Hola, hola*?" Yasmin called, rapping a knuckle on the front entrance.

"We're here," Jessica shouted from the front step.

"Great, just great. Jessica is here too." Carlos turned and limped hurriedly towards his bedroom.

"Yasmin. Jessica. Come in, come in," Pedro said as he flung the front door wide open, displaying Carlos' barely covered pale brown ass as it disappeared through the doorway.

Jessica noticed the flash of toned flesh. "Hmmm, nice butt. Guess he wasn't expecting us so soon," she said, hugging Pedro and giving him a friendly buss on the cheek.

Sparky rushed to Jessica, planting his front paws on her knees, his tail in full helicopter-mode, circling around and around. Jessica bent to scratch his ears and chin, "My smart little man."

Yasmin wrapped Pedro in a fierce hug, giving him an affectionate kiss on the cheek, "Thank you. Thank you for finding Carlos." She released Pedro and wrapped her arms around Diego. "I can't thank you guys enough."

Diego answered, simply, "He's our best friend."

Yasmin released her embrace, and Jessica grabbed Diego for a rib squishing hug. "So good to see everyone safe and sound," Jessica said.

Antonio stood, his arms open wide, "And me? What about me?"

"We couldn't have done it without you," Yasmin said, embracing him and kissing him on the cheek. "Thank you so very much."

Jessica stood a few feet back and smiled boldly at Antonio. "Yes, thank you. But we should have been there."

"You never give up," the cop responded with a wide grin and a laugh.

"No, I don't." she agreed, then turned her attention to Sparky. "Did you miss me, sweetie?" She cooed to the pooch as he pressed against her leg. "You've been spending too much time with these big smelly men."

"I'm not smelly anymore," Carlos said, joining the group. He had tossed on a pair of khaki shorts and deep blue t-shirt. His bare feet pattered quietly on the tile floor.

"Carlos! You said you had just a *small bump* on the head. You look like you have been run over by a truck." Yasmin hurried over, reaching to embrace him.

"Easy, *carina*, easy," he said. "I'm a little scuffed up."

"So, come on. Tell us what happened, everything up to now." Jessica prompted, lifting a cold beer from the refrigerator and waggling it in front of the others. "Anyone else want one?"

"Not me thanks," Diego checked his pockets for keys, then gave the women each a peck on the cheek. "I've got to go or Cristina will divorce me. She's at home with the kids and has only a vague idea of what happened with José." He waved goodbye and headed out the front door to his Jeep.

The women turned to stare at the remaining men. "Come on, give. We've been worried to death," Yasmin demanded.

Carlos carefully lowered himself into his favorite comfortable chair, lifting first one leg then the other to the footstool. Earlier the men had decided to tell Yasmin and Jessica the almost true story, including the part about José, but omitting Diego's soccer kick. "Okay, I'll start with what happened after I last saw you on New Year's Eve, but I desperately need another *cerveza*."

Jessica reached back into the refrigerator, grabbed a beer, twisted off the cap, and handed it to him. "Talk!"

A beam of sunlight pushed through a gap between the curtains. Carlos shifted his weight away from his aching left knee and the pain in his ribs, rolling gingerly towards the center of the bed. A tangle of dark curly hair poked out from under a sheet pulled high on a lean shoulder. Yasmin. He had no memory of going to bed, much less of Yasmin joining him. Trailing a finger on her cheek, he leaned over and softly kissed her.

A green eye popped open, examining him. "Ah, so you've rejoined the land of the living," she said, turning on her back.

Leaning in, Carlos kissed her again more urgently. "Mmmm. Did we have fun last night?" he asked, his eyebrows dancing suggestively.

"Fun? You were dead to the world about twenty minutes after your parents arrived." Yasmin's mouth quirked, "Pedro and Antonio carried you into the bedroom, and your mom insisted on undressing you. I'm pretty sure she thought I might take advantage of you in your weakened state."

"Well did you? Take advantage of me? I hope."

"No, I prefer my lovers to be conscious." Twisting over, she swung her legs onto the tile floor. "I have to pee. Don't go away."

The turquoise colored t-shirt, that Carlos recognized as one of his, grazed the bottom of her butt. A little tent poked up under the bedding as he felt his body respond. Morning sex. His all-time favorite, right after late-night sex, make-up sex, and it's-raining sex. His ribs hurt like hell. He was cut and scraped, but with a little extra care they could probably figure out a way to have a little fun before going to work.

Chapter 42

January 5th Mid-morning

"We need to talk," Yasmin said, as she climbed back into bed, stiffly propping her back against the headboard and clasping her hands in her lap.

Carlos could feel his morning erection wilt at the ominous sound of the words, 'we need to talk'. It was woman-code for any number of sticky situations, such as, I want a divorce, or I'm pregnant, or my mother is coming to stay for six months. He and Yasmin weren't married so no divorce. They had only recently become sexually involved and took precautions, so not likely pregnant, unless he had super-sperm. Her mom and dad lived in Mérida and seemed to be happily married, so probably not that one either.

"Okay," he said, propping himself up on one elbow to watch her face. "What would you like to talk about?" *And why couldn't we have had some fun before we had this discussion?*

She remained silent, refusing to meet his gaze.

"Yassy, what's wrong?" He reached out a hand, gently running it over her slim leg. "I vaguely remember you telling me something about a fire at your house. Do you need a place to live?"

"No. It's not that," she blurted as the tears overflowed her eyelids. "It's my fault you were kidnapped."

"That's silly," he said, easing himself into a sitting position beside her. "How could it be your fault?"

Turning her tear-filled eyes to look at him, she said, "Kirk wanted the treasure."

"Yes, I know. Patterson said he thought Diego or Pedro took it from him. They don't have the treasure, and neither do I."

"Jess and I have it," she said. "Sparky found the bag a few days ago."

"What? How?"

"We went for a walk in Hacienda Mundaca Park on December 31st. Sparky must have recognized Jessica's scent on the bag." She plucked at the sheet, twisting it with her fingers. "He pulled the sack out from under a bush, and we hid it in my laptop safe. After the fire at my place, we moved it to Jessica's house."

When he didn't respond, she stopped her fidgeting and looked at him, "Are you angry at me, Carlos?"

He ran his hand through his hair as a delaying tactic, "No, I'm not angry, Yasmin." He hesitated for a long moment before continuing, "Concerned, but not angry." The set expression on his face said otherwise.

"I'm sorry we didn't tell you, but Patterson grabbed you before we had a chance to say anything."

"No harm done." He swung his feet onto the floor, offering her a conciliatory smile. "I'm going to take a shower and get dressed. I have to check on the restaurant." He patted the bed, "Stay as long as you like. The coffee pot is all set to go, just flick the switch."

Yasmin watched as he limped towards the bathroom, holding one arm tight against his side. "Oh, damn it," she whispered.

As the shower started, Yasmin made up her mind. It was time to return to her own home to get her life sorted out. She slid off the bed, hurriedly pulling on her shorts and top, and slipping her feet into her sandals. She quickly searched in the kitchen for something to write a note with. Finding a pen, she tested it on a scrap of paper, then discarded it—dried out. A stub of pencil rested on top of the microwave along with a partially used note book. It would have to do. She hastily scratched a note, apologizing once again and telling him she would be at work at her regular time today. *If I still have a job*, she thought, quietly pulling the front door closed.

Stepping onto the scooter, Yasmin stuck the key in the ignition, settled her helmet, and pulled away from the parking spot. Fifteen minutes later, as she neared Jessica's address, she changed her mind about going to her home. She pulled the moto to the curb and set the kickstand. She needed to talk to Jessica right now. It wasn't a conversation for the phone.

Chapter 43

January 5th Mid-day

The remnants of his meal scattered in front of him, Carlos sipped his third cup of coffee at the *Loco Lobo*. He felt half-way human again. His first two hours at the restaurant had been consumed with answering questions from his employees.

Questions about his sister Marianna's supposed health issues; she had recovered nicely.

Questions about his limp; he'd answered with a fib, saying he'd fallen off a moto in Mérida.

Questions about what to do about this little problem or that one. No one seemed to have any idea that he had been abducted.

Jessica and Yasmin had done a great job looking after the *Loco Lobo.* It had survived just fine without him, but the staff were looking for reassurances that everything was returning to normal.

Yasmin's confession this morning about the treasure had caught him off-guard. It wasn't her fault, but he was irritated that his life and the lives of his friends, plus young

José, had been put in danger because that damnable pirate treasure just kept popping up.

Across the table, Antonio swallowed the last bite of a double cheeseburger, washing it down with a swig of Coke. "I hate to say it, *hermano*, but I have to catch the next passenger ferry. My flight home leaves at two this afternoon."

"So soon? We haven't had a lot of time to visit," Carlos said, a sincere smile lighting his face. "I was planning to buy you a fancy dinner tonight with lots of wine and tequila, as a thank you."

Antonio shook his head regretfully, "I have already told my boss that I will be at work tomorrow morning," adding with a grin, "and my Luisa misses me."

"I really appreciate you coming." Carlos said. Feeling the emotion well up in his chest, he swallowed and stopped talking.

"You would have done the same for me," Antonio replied. Then he glanced around in a mannerism that was very familiar to Carlos. He seemed to be checking that the staff was occupied, and no customers were seated nearby. "About those little trinkets the ladies have..." he quietly whispered.

Carlos' face clouded. "Yasmin told me the story this morning," he said. "The events of this past week were all because of those miserable bits and pieces." He didn't say the word treasure, cautious of being overheard despite Antonio's recent check for eavesdroppers.

Antonio nodded, "True." He leveled his gaze at Carlos, "As far as I am concerned those things don't exist, just tell the ladies to be careful. They could end up in another big mess, either legally or with another low-life trying to make easy money."

Carlos cocked an eyebrow. "Tell them?" he snorted. "Suggest maybe, but tell? Not going to work."

Antonio stood, pulling his small soft-sided travel bag out from under the table. "Well for what it's worth, it's just a word of warning."

"*Si, claro*." Carlos nodded, agreeing with the need for discretion. "Let me give you a ride to the Ultramar," he said, slowly pushing himself to his feet.

"It's only a three-block walk. I'm good, and you've got things to do here."

Protecting his sore ribs with one arm, Carlos wrapped the other arm over his friend's shoulders. "Love ya, *mi hermano*."

"Same to you. Take care of yourself, and come visit Luisa and me soon."

"Si, I will, I promise," he agreed.

Walking towards the street, Antonio waved goodbye over his shoulder.

Carlos said to his back, "Give my love to your family. And a kiss for Luisa."

As Antonio disappeared from sight, Carlos picked up the new phone that he had purchased this morning and thumbed in Yasmin's number.

"We need to talk," he said; the irony of his choice of words caused the corner of his mouth to twitch.

Chapter 44

January 5th Early afternoon

Sparky sat on the floor beside Jessica, his human-like eyes tracking her every move. Her dog was once again basking in his celebrity status, although he wasn't as famous as when he uncovered the pirate treasure a few months ago. Only the tight group of friends knew the entire story about Carlos' kidnapping, little José being held at knife point, and Sparky helping to save him. Everyone else had been told the sanitized version of the story, how the State Police responded to an anonymous tip about a dangerous American killer seen on the island. The fugitive who was wanted in connection with several murders in Florida had unfortunately slipped and dropped to his death while trying to avoid recapture. Neither they nor any of their friends wanted more notoriety.

For now, at least, anything that Sparky wanted, Sparky got, including fillet mignon for his supper this evening. What a little *divo*. Jessica grinned at his sloppy smile, then swung her attention to the source of tension in the room—Carlos. He wasn't happy.

He had phoned Yasmin, asking if everyone could meet at Jessica's for a few minutes. He wanted to talk to them before they started their afternoon shift at the restaurant. Earlier in the day Yasmin had told Jessica about her strained conversation with Carlos. The women had half-heartedly agreed to the meeting, certain they knew what he wanted to talk about.

"What's up, Carlos?" Jessica reluctantly asked.

Leaning forward, with his forearms braced on his bent knees, Carlos replied, "I'm concerned. I'm concerned about the safety of you and Yasmin. And I am concerned about the safety of your friends, your families, and our families."

Jessica flipped a dismissive hand in the air, "If you are referring to the treasure, don't worry," Jessica retorted, annoyed by the stiff expression on his face.

"Jess," Diego began, "just hear the guy out...please." He held up one hand in a wait-a-minute motion.

"We gave it away," Yasmin blurted, before Jessica could snap out another retort. "We gave it all away this morning."

"What?"

"Are you kidding me?"

"Who did you give it to?"

"Just chill. You keep tossing all of these questions at us and we can't get a word in edgewise," Jessica replied. She felt guilty for problems the treasure had caused but wished they could have kept at least a bauble or two. She and Yasmin had discussed the problem at length this morning and decided it all had to go, every damn little bit.

"We think it is cursed, or at least bad luck for us." Yasmin circled her hand, indicating the group. "Misfortune has followed this treasure for centuries. Pirates killed four hundred people when they looted Veracruz in 1683. Then last November, Kirk Patterson attacked Jessica and me over a few items that Sparky had dug up," she pointed at the faint scar under her chin, "leaving me this reminder of his visit."

She looked at Carlos, adding softly, "But more recently, he abducted you, Carlos, and threatened to kill both you and little José. That would have been unbearable." She paused, pulling in a deep breath, "If he had succeeded in grabbing Antonio's gun, who knows who else would be hurt or killed." She shook her head, "It's the cause of bad things happening to the people we care the most about."

Jessica held out her empty hands, and simply said, "So we gave it away."

Pedro's face was knotted in puzzlement as he asked, "How did you give away a fortune in jewels and religious artifacts without arousing suspicion?"

"We anonymously donated it to the Isla Mujeres orphanage, the one in Rancho Viejo," Yasmin said.

"The one Rubén supports?" Pedro asked, his eyebrows quirking up.

"*Si*," Yasmin confirmed, "Casa Hogar San José De La Inmaculada. They look after kids who have little hope of a better life." Her expression brightened as she added, "Tomorrow is the annual Día de Reyes party for the youngsters at his restaurant. With our little bit of financial assistance, it should be a memorable party this year."

Carlos' face relaxed into a warm smile, his eyes seeking Yasmin's. "Well, that's a surprise and a huge relief. Thank you. Thank you so much, *mi amor*," he said.

"Maybe good can overcome the bad karma of the treasure," Jessica said, shrugging her shoulders. "At least that's what we were hoping when we donated it." She wasn't convinced that the treasure was bad luck, but it certainly hadn't brought them good luck either.

"Except that beautiful cross. It didn't seem right to just give it away," Yasmin added with a sly smile. "We left it in the collection box of the Capilla de Guadalupe, for the padre to find."

Carlos slowly pushed himself upright and pulled Yasmin into a careful hug. With laughter in his voice, he said, "That will be an interesting mystery for the padre to puzzle over."

El Fin

Hola amigos y amigas

Pardon my lack of Spanish. I keep trying to learn, but every night while I am sleeping the words leak out of my brain and onto the pillow.

In a perfect world, I would have written this story in Spanish or in this case Isla-Spanish which is a colorful mix of local expressions and a bit of Mayan tossed in for added flavor.

However, most of my readers are English speaking. So, for the purpose of this story, the local folks are fluent in both Spanish and English, especially the cuss words.

I chose to *italicize* only a few of the less familiar Spanish expressions.

Like every self-published writer, I rely heavily on recommendations and reviews to sell my books. If you enjoyed reading any of my *Isla Mujeres Mysteries* or my *Death in the Vineyards* novels please leave a review on Amazon, Goodreads, Bookbub, Facebook or Twitter. Tell your friends, tell your family, or anyone who will listen. Word of mouth is enormously helpful.

If you come across an annoying blunder, please contact me via one of my social media accounts and I will make it disappear.

Facebook @ Lynda L Lock
Instagram @ Lynda Lock
Amazon @ Lynda L Lock
Bookbub @ Lynda L Lock
Goodreads @ Lynda L Lock
A Writer's Life blog

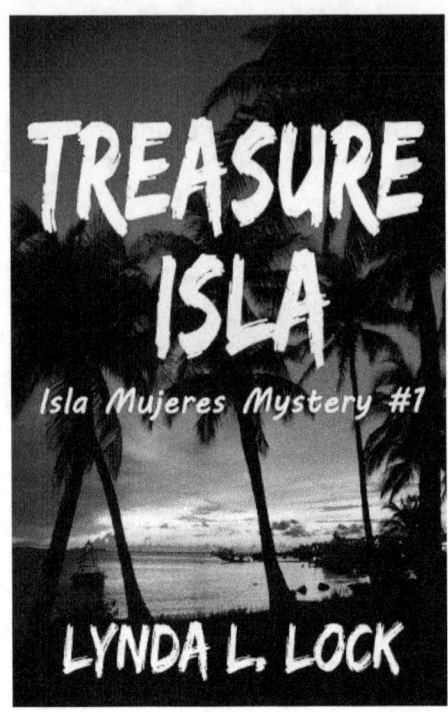

And there are more Isla Mujeres Mysteries!

Treasure Isla Book #1

Treasure Isla is a humorous Caribbean adventure set on Isla Mujeres, a tiny island off the eastern coast of Mexico. Two twenty-something women find themselves in possession of a seemingly authentic treasure map, which leads them on a chaotic search for buried treasure while navigating the dangers of too much tequila, disreputable men, and a killer. And there is a dog, a lovable rescue mutt.

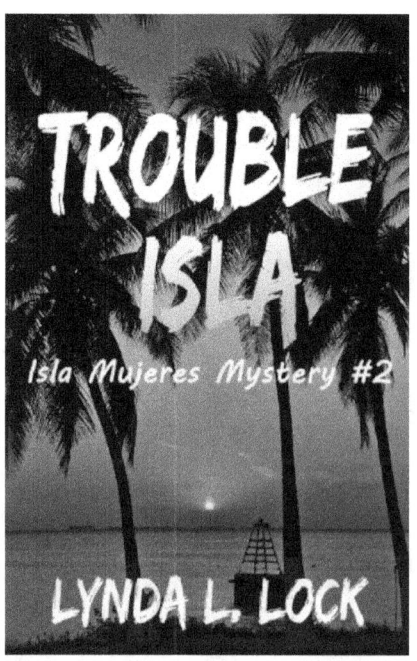

Trouble Isla Book #2

"This pair of leading ladies are fun to immerse in for an afternoon escape. The character development is richly layered and entertaining. The stakes are also enjoyably high, and the action sequences will keep readers voraciously flipping pages. Trouble Isla is a quick, unpredictable read. Bringing this small Caribbean island to life, and populating it with vivid characters that will continue to carry this series forward, Lynda L. Lock has created a uniquely colorful mystery." Self-Publishing Review, ★★★★

Tormenta Isla Book #3

A mysterious disappearance of a local man and the looming threat of multiple hurricanes headed toward the peaceful Caribbean island of Isla Mujeres creates havoc in the lives of Jessica, her friends and her rescue mutt, Sparky. - Diego held up his smartphone and silently showed her the screen, pointing at the NOAA graphics.

Her eyes opened wide in surprise as she looked at the screen, then a frown crinkled her brow. "Really? Three hurricanes?"

"*Si*," he responded, "Pablo, Rebekah, y Sebastien."

Temptation Isla Book #4

Rafael Fernandez leaned forward resting his elbows on the polished wood, tapping his finger-tips together. "Take them all out! At the reception." He said, sweeping his right hand in a side-ways motion as if he was knocking a pile of papers from his desk to the floor.

"As you wish, Don Rafael." Alfonso Fuentes' jaw muscle twitched with tension.

"You don't agree?" Fernandez snarled.

Alfonso paused momentarily considering his next words. He had to get this exactly right or he would, at the very least, be demoted to the riskiest tasks or in the worse-case scenario killed for insubordination.

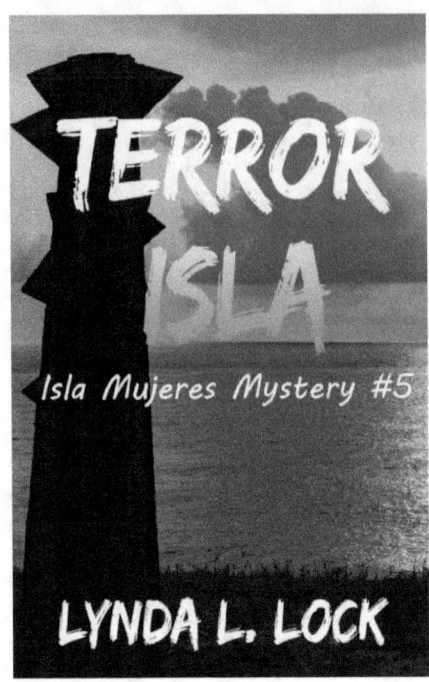

Terror Isla Book #5

Isla Mujeres, a tiny island paradise in the Caribbean Sea, is rocked by a power struggle between a Mexican cartel and a Romanian gang as they battle for control of the illegitimate ATM skimming. Big changes are coming for Carlos and Yasmin, while Jessica Sanderson fends off an angry lover from her past. Sparky, Jessica's stocky beach mutt is once again at the center of another Sparky-situation.

"I want a super-hero cape. A red one," Diego Avalos said. "I am feeling very underappreciated."

"In Jessica's opinion, Sparky is the super-hero with the red cape. We're just his minions doing his bidding," Pedro rejoined. "I'll pick you up in ten minutes."

Twisted Isla Book #6

Death stalks the annual Island Time Music Festival. Nashville musicians and songwriters flock to the tropical island of Isla Mujeres to raise funds for the Little Yellow School House. Jessica and her keen-nosed beach-mutt Sparky are thrown into another murder mystery.

Sergeant Ramirez held up his palm with his fingers spread wide, "That's the fifth."

"Fifth what?" Asked Mike Lyons."

"Body," answered Ramirez, his eyes sweeping to Jessica's face, "that we've had to question señorita Sanderson about."

"Really?" Mike lobbed a startled look at Jessica.

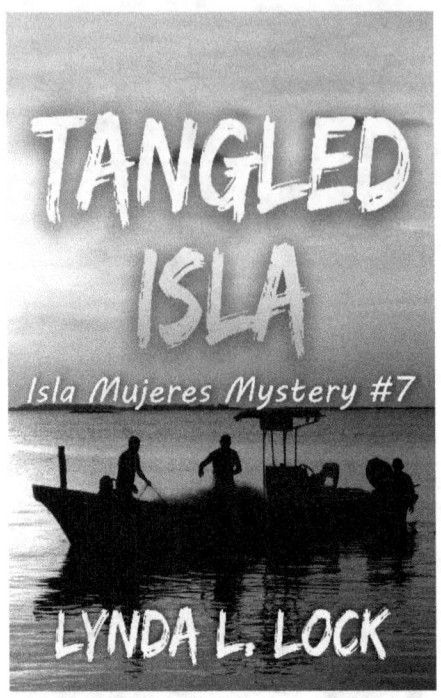

Tangled Isla Book #7

Has an unidentified killer of several Florida women relocated to the tropical paradise of Isla Mujeres?

Leading up to the busiest time of the year on Isla Mujeres, four young women similar in appearance to the Florida victims, are unaccounted for and have been reported as missing by concerned friends.

Longing for a reunion with her island friends, Jessica Sanderson returns to Mexico on a solo visit, leaving her partner Mike Lyons with the challenging task of babysitting her legendary and finicky dog, Sparky.

When Jessica arrives on the island she is persuaded to participate in the annual children's parade, wearing the Minnie Mouse costume. The parade is disrupted by an unexplained event, and Jessica becomes entangled in the mystery of the missing women.

Will Jessica be able to solve this mystery without the help of Sparky, her famous clue-finding pooch? Grab your copy today to find out!

CORKED #1 Death in the Vineyards

Love, lust, and loot in the affluent world of wine and wineries.

CORKED, is the newest murder mystery from the author of the exciting Isla Mujeres Mysteries. Murder follows Jessica Sanderson and her detective dog Sparky as they relocate from their Caribbean paradise in Mexico to the Okanagan wine country in Canada. On Isla Mujeres, big changes are coming for Jessica's friends as the COVID19 virus gains momentum. Leaving her beloved island Jessica follows her new love interest, Mike Lyons, into a new adventure.

SMASHED #2 Death in the Vineyards

Some people can convince themselves they can do no wrong.

While wildfires ravage the Okanagan Valley, Jessica Sanderson and her love interest Mike Lyons battle to save two wineries; one from the massive wildfire that is threatening homes and businesses in Okanagan Falls, and the other from economic disaster and the sudden death of their winemaker.

In *SMASHED*, Jessica and her Mexi-mutt Sparky find themselves in the middle of a sticky situation. In this highly-anticipated sequel to *CORKED*, inquisitive Jessica and the amazing nose of Sparky are once again caught up in a police investigation.

CRUSHED #3 Death in the Vineyards

Sometimes tragedy strikes from a clear blue sky.

While creating a new life for themselves in the Okanagan Valley's wine region, Jessica Sanderson and Mike Lyons become entangled in another unexpected death.

CRUSHED takes us a wild ride of intertwined tragedies, family secrets, and substance abuse, while RCMP Corporal Caitlin Smith races to solve the murder and unravel the surrounding mystery. Will Jessica's Mexican beach mutt, Sparky, and his keen nose again help with the investigation?

Grab your copy today, and join the adventure.

Acknowledgements

Writing is a solitary obsession with hours spent creating, considering, and correcting the words on the computer screen.

However, I have had assistance from some amazing people:

- Tony Garcia, for the beautiful photos on the covers of three of my novels.
- Carmen Amato, mystery writer and creator of the Emilia Cruz Detective Series, designed the cover template for this book and the sequels.
- Freddy Medina, Eva Velázquez, Javier Martinez, Marla Bainbridge, Patricio Yam Dzul, plus Aida Yolanda Pérez Martín are cherished friends who are always willing to share their stories of life on Isla Mujeres—before it became a popular tourist destination.
- Apache (Isauro Martinez Jr.) is another one of my go-to-friends when I am searching for specific information about the island.
- Sid Hollander of the Azatlan group who contacted Professor Jesús Guillermo Kantún Rivera for the Mayan name of the god of turtles, Itzam K'an Ahk.
- Brad and Tiffany Wareing of Barlito's Bakery and Market Café for their humorous anecdote about the iguana in the sewer.
- Manuscript and proofreaders include, Lawrie Lock, Linda Grierson, Richard Grierson, Rob Goth, Julie Andrews Goth, Shirley Andrews, Carolina Sanders, Sue McDonald Lo, Janice Carlisle Rodgers and Kim Lawton.
- And a very special thanks to Editor Michael Rowley, for helping me pull this story together. Any and all remaining mistakes are mine.

Thank you, thank you, and thank you all!

About the author

Born in a British Columbia Canada gold mining community that is now essentially a ghost town, Lynda has had a diverse, some might say eccentric, working career. Her job history includes bank clerk, antique store owner, ambulance attendant, volunteer firefighter, supervisor of the SkyTrain transit control center, partner in a bed & breakfast, partner in a microbrewery, and hotel manager. The adventure and the experience were always more important than the paycheck.

Writing has always been in the background of her life, starting with travel articles for a local newspaper, an unpublished novel written before her fortieth birthday, and articles for a Canadian safety magazine.

When she and her husband, Lawrie Lock, retired to Isla Mujeres, Mexico in 2008, they started a weekly blog, Notes from Paradise, to keep friends and family up to date on their newest adventure.

Needing something more to keep her active mind occupied, Lynda and island friend Diego Medina self-published two bilingual books for children, The Adventures of Thomas the Cat / Las Aventuras de Tómas el Gato plus The Adventures of Thomas and Sparky / Las Aventuras de Tómas y Sparky.

Well, one thing led to another and Lynda created and self-published the Isla Mujeres Mystery series, set on the island in the Caribbean Sea where they lived. Following the death of Lawrie in 2018, she and Sparky remained in Mexico until the COVID-19 pandemic became a reality.

In March of 2020 Lynda and Sparky decided to return to wine country in BC Canada. Her new Death in the Vineyard series combines two things dear to her heart: Canada and good wine.

The legal stuff

- Most of the characters and events in this book are fictional except Martiniana Gomez Pantoja, nicknamed *La Trigueña,* and the two captains, Laurens de Graaf and Fermin Mundaca.
- Island resident and friend Tony Garcia, is real.
- Javi's Cantina on Juarez Avenue exists. It is one of our favorite locations to have a tasty dinner and listen to live music.
- Isla Brewing Company - Cerveza Isla makes delicious handcrafted ales that are available in a few select restaurants.
- Jessica Sanderson is a product of my imagination but like me, was born in BC Canada and she has a soft spot for critters of any type including mammals, reptiles, amphibians, or insects.
- Carlos Mendoza shares a few characteristics with my husband Lawrie; a good sense of humor, the love of dancing, plus the appreciation of Rolex watches and expensive cars.
- The *Loco Lobo Restaurant* is completely fictitious, it is not based on any particular location or restaurant.
- Any other resemblance to persons, whether living or dead is strictly coincidental. All rights reserved.
- No part of this book may be reproduced or transmitted in any form by any means, electronic or mechanical, including photocopying, recording, scanning to a computer disk, or by any information storage and retrieval system, without express permission in writing from the publisher.

Trouble Isla
Published by Lynda L. Lock
Copyright 2017
All rights reserved.
Electronic: ISBN 978-0-9936203-4-8
Paperback: ISBN 978-0-9936203-5-5
Hardcover: ISBN 978-1-7389616-4-1

Spanish expressions

Bruja del Mar – Literally witch of the sea, Sea Witch
Carina – urban slang for a funny, gorgeous girlfriend
Casita – small house
Casa – house
Claro or claro que sí – agreement, of course
Cómo está? – How are you?
Con permiso – to move around or past a person
Cuchi-cuchi – humorous euphemism for sex
Don or Doña – respectful title used with the first name
Hermano – brother, or any male who is like a brother
Hermana – sister, or any female who is like a sister
Hijo de la chingada – crude curse, son of a bitch
Hola – hi or hello
Hombre – man
La Trigueña – The young woman Mundaca loved
Loco Lobo – Crazy Wolf, also El Loco Lobo
Maldito – darn, damn
Mama – mom   Mami – mommy
Mande? – The person didn't hear you.
Más o menos – more or less
Mi amor – my love
Mierda – swear word, shit
Mordidita – bribe, literally a little bite
Motos – motor scooters, motorbikes
Niña(s) – girl or girls
Niño(s) – boy or boys, can also mean children
Papa – dad   Papi – daddy
Pendejo – swear word
Que pasa – what's happening
Que pasó – what happened
Rapido – rapid, fast
Tia – auntie, or an older female who is like an aunt
Tio – uncle, or an older male who is like an uncle
Topes – speed bumps

www.ingramcontent.com/pod-product-compliance
Lightning Source LLC
Chambersburg PA
CBHW060310260626
47160CB00007B/2558